Surgeons of Terror 6

Al-Qaida 3763

Ron Wootters

"SOT 6 – Al-Qaida 3763," by Ron Wootters. ISBN 978-1-60264-902-6 (softcover) and ISBN 978-1-60264-903-3 (electronic verison).

Published 2011 by Virtualbookworm.com Publishing Inc., P.O. Box 9949, College Station, TX , 77842,US.

Manufactured in the United States of America.

To:

**All U.S. Intelligence and Armed Forces
Personnel
Past, Present & Future
Thank You**

Edited by:
Lisa DiGloria
Book Ink Editing
www.bookink.com

In Memory Of:

All U.S. and allied personnel who lost
their lives serving their country

Continued Special Thanks To The Medical Community:

Dr. David DiPietro M.D. Family Practice
Dr. Paul Spiro M.D. Family Practice
Dr. Joseph Curci M.D. General Surgery
Dr. Bruce Derrick M.D. General Surgery
Dr. Brian M. Pellini M.D. General Surgery
Dr. Bruce Applestein M.D. Cardiology
Dr. Michael Mooradd M.D. Cardiology
Dr. Steven Guidera M.D. Cardiology
Dr. Randy Metcalf M.D. Cardiothoracic Surgery
Dr. Joseph Auteri M.D. Cardiothoracic Surgery
Dr. James H. Wright M.D. Anesthesiology
Dr. Robert O'Connor M.D. Anesthesiology
Dr. Steve McDonald M.D. Anesthesiology
Dr. Jon Walheim M.D. Internal Medicine
Dr. Joseph Shrager M.D. Dermatology
Dr. Robert J. Willard M.D. Dermatology, Mohs
Dr. Cynthia Matossian M.D. Opthalmology
Dr. June E. Grutzmacher M.D. Ophthalmology
Dr. Steven Flashner M.D. Urology
Dr. Melchiore Vernace M.D. Nephrology
Dr. Robert H. Hale M.D. Gastroenterology
Dr. Timothy Orphanides M.D. Gastroenterology
Dr. Joseph K. Kim M.D. Gastroenterology
Dr. Frank A. Welsch M.D. Pulmonary Disease
Dr. Les Szekely M.D. Pulmonary Disease
Dr. Stanford Gittlen M.D. Pulmonary Disease
Dr. Gregory Gallant M.D Orthopedic Surgery
Dr. David M. Junkin Jr. M.D Orthopedic Surgery
Dr. Douglas Boylan M.D. Orthopedic Surgery
Dr. J. Michael Whitaker M.D. Orthopedic Surgery
Dr. David A. Silberman M.D. Plastic Surgery
Dr. Daniel J. Coletta M.D. Gynecology
Dr. Laurie Gerstein M.D. Gynecology; Gynecologic Surgery
Dr. Douglas Nadel M.D. Otolaryngology

Dr. Lynn M. Azzara M.P.D Podiatry
Dr. Richard Rathgeber D.O. Emergency Medicine
Dr. Robert Linkenheimer D.O. Emergency Medicine
Dr. Mark Choi M.D. Emergency Medicine
Dr. Lawrence Brilliant M.D. Emergency Medicine
Dr. Charles Fasano D.O. Emergency Medicine
Emergency Department Doylestown Hospital
The Heart Institute Doylestown Hospital
The Cath Lab Doylestown Hospital
Cardiac Rehab Center Doylestown Hospital
Xray, CT Scan, MRI Doylestown Hospital
GI/Endoscopy Doylestown Hospital
Physician Assistant's, Labs, Nurses, Staff at Doylestown
Hospital
Mr. Rich Reif and the Board of Directors at Doylestown
Hospital
Dr. Larry A. Ufberg DMD Endodontist
Dr. Mark Bydalek, D.M.D Dentistry
Dr. Richard Gruber D.D.S Dentistry
Neil Letcavage Physical Therapist
Richard L. Stoneking, Physical Therapist

All Good Nurses Everywhere

Lambertville—New Hope Ambulance and Rescue Squad
'When the siren calls the Squad is already on the way'

Doctors, PA's, Nurses and Staffs at:
Buckingham Family Medicine
Joseph J. Curci, M.D., F.A.C.S.
Central Bucks Cardiology
Bucks County Cardiothoracic Surgery
The Heart Institute
Central Bucks Urology
Nephrology-Hypertension Specialist
Central Bucks Specialists Limited

Doylestown Health Gastroenterology
Bucks County Medical Association / Pulmonary
June E. Grutzmacher, M.D., F.A.C.S.
Orthopaedic Specialty Center
Doylestown Orthopedic Specialists
Doylestown Internal Medicine Associates
Doylestown Gynecology
Matossian Eye Associates
VIAA Surgical Associates
Dermatology and Mohs Surgery Center. PC
Plastic Surgery Associates
Doylestown Surgical Center
Ent Associates of Bucks County
Lynn M. Azzara, MPD
Pennsylvania Endodontic Specialists
Mark Bydalek, DMD
Stoneking PT & Wellness Center
Nova Care—Doylestown, PA

Rosemary and I are very fortunate to live in an area where we have access to such excellent medical care.

Prologue

Only a few at the very top level of Al-Qaida were in attendance at a meeting being held at one of their strongholds in North Africa.

Ayman al Zawahiri, the man known to the world as Al-Qaida's number two man—but in actuality, had been number one since 1998—had called the meeting and was addressing the group.

"Phase three of our plan is now completed and we will be moving onto the fourth and final phase, but first, I would like to address the reasoning behind the Brotherhood's decision to allow information to leak out concerning Osama's whereabouts.

"As you all know, Osama Bin Laden was actually more of a finance individual than a true terrorist, but after 9/11, he became the face of terrorism and the main focus of our enemies, allowing others to move more freely. To most people outside of this room, he was Al-Qaida and his killing will generate more finances, manpower, and a cry for vengeance.

"Our organization has been degraded badly and the sacrifice of one of our own was a small price to pay, especially when considering what Al-Qaida will gain.

"All of the information we allowed to be found on Osama's PC and storage devices should send U.S. Intelligence looking into areas we have long since abandoned. If the professional intelligence people in the U.S. start to question the validity of the information obtained at the compound, they will be overridden by the politically appointed intelligence dogs who will insist for political reasons that the information is authentic.

"I would like to address another issue," Zawahiri continued. "Most of the financing for all four phases of our next planned attack was provided by our brothers here in North Africa. They escorted and protected drug trafficking, but since drugs are haram (taboo) to Islam, I want to make it clear that they had no direct involvement with the drugs. They provided security for over fifty tons of cocaine from Latin America and over thirty tons of Afghan Heroin passing through Africa and felt justified since it was on its way to poison the west.

"Now onto phase four," Zawahiri said, returning to the primary topic of the meeting. "As you all know, our brothers in Afghanistan, Pakistan, and in other parts of the world have been paying a heavy price and it would seem to the world at large we are totally defensive and recent events would reinforce that belief, but in fact, we have been planning an event that will rock The Great Satan.

"Total security must be maintained and the entire plan will only be known to those at the highest levels. However, if called upon, you will be expected to assist at all cost. Without question, this attack will be the largest we have ever undertaken, even surpassing 9/11.

"All strategies have been reviewed many times to correct flaws, tests have been conducted, and harmless dry runs have been carried out in the belly of the Great Satan."

"Planning is now completed, dry runs have all been very successful, and we are now prepared to move into the final stage of our next great attack. If all goes as planned, there will be hundreds of thousands of Americans affected by this attack and the name Al-Qaida will again be heard and feared around the world!" Zawahiri said, intentionally raising his voice to arouse the members at the meeting who responded with absolute fanaticism.

Chapter 1

JJ Stone was sitting in the kitchen of his country home enjoying his second cup of coffee when General Mac entered in search of his first morning shot of caffeine. With the exception of Top Kiner, JJ and Mac were the early birds of the group, usually already having had coffee and were engaged in conversation before the others were up and about.

JJ had converted his New Jersey country home and barn into what seemed to be a very upscale and exclusive bed and breakfast. However, it was actually home base, AKA The Barn, for the anti-terrorist teams he had formed in 2001.

Once Mac had gotten his coffee and was seated at the table, JJ started the morning conversation with, "It's around that time we usually go through our review process for the Board and Teams, but I'm considering a change to the process. Instead of the Board doing the Teams' review, maybe it would be better if you and JC performed that task and then reported your findings back to the Board?"

"Sounds like a plan," Mac agreed.

"As in the past, you and I will still perform the Board review," JJ added, as he reached for a pad and pencil that was on the table. He started writing down the names of the Board members. John Howard, President of Zerk Pharmaceutical; Jeff Dawson, President of International Oil; Gil Dunn, President of Van Corcoven Firearms Company and former DDO at CIA; Admiral Fox (Foxie) retired, Navy Intel and former Navy Seal; Charles Wilson, President of Wilson Explosives Company.

With that complete, the two men evaluated each man and discussed any possible weaknesses or problems, and as usual, found none.

Not only were the Board members responsible for the financial and logistical needs for the Teams and Projects, they also made the initial Project selections and on more than one occasion, participated in them up close and personal.

The point of the pencil JJ was holding rested on the last name he had written on the pad when he said, "General Mac, USMC retired. Oh, that's you," JJ said with fake surprise. "Now what is it you do again? Aren't you the duty Pecker Checker or something like that?" he inquired. He then stood up and quickly walked away from the table.

General Mac was caught off-guard, but quickly recovered and followed to continue their never-ending verbal battle.

Since it was still early, Mac decided to talk with JC about the review process prior to breakfast. He left the house and walked toward the big renovated barn where JC and the Team resided when not on a Project or on leave. *Time does fly,* Mac thought to himself. *It's hard to believe the Team has been operational for the past ten years.*

Upon entering The Barn, Mac proceeded to what everyone referred to as the Com Shack, knowing he would probably find JC diddling with a new gizmo.

Their relationship went way back to their Marine Corps years and the reason Mac recommended JC. After JJ and the Board approved his recommendation, JC and Mac selected and recruited the entire Team. Once that was completed, Mac recommended Top Kiner who then recruited what they now call the House Team who are responsible for maintaining home base and security, but somehow seem to get involved in Projects away from Home Base, a fact that had given JJ three more people to worry about during past Projects.

Since Mac had already given JC a heads up about the reviewing of the Teams, he was prepared and ready to start as both men took a seat. When the Teams were formed, each member was given a code name and was always addressed by that code name, so Mac started the process with, "JC, Team Leader, retired Marine Corps Colonel, pilot, expert with weapons, and the main gizmo man. Are you going anywhere?" Mac inquired.

"Not anytime soon," JC replied.

"Moving on," Mac continued and the duo reviewed each Team Member. Blue Jay, field Team Leader, contract type, former Marine Corps, and CIA. Bean, contract type, prior Army Airborne Ranger, Special Forces, and CIA. Benz, Japanese, expert in martial arts, been in the contract business part-time for many years. Panda, Filipino, also expert in martial arts, part-time contractor, regular occupation: is an engineering consultant. Check, Arab, explosives, part-time contractor, owns a Middle Eastern restaurant. Tic, Cuban, explosives, part-time contractor, regular occupation is a stockbroker. Bris, French, primarily a contractor, but also an artist and a good one. Pru, English, contractor, long-range shooter. Met, German, also a contractor, long-range shooter. Air Jockey, contractor, can fly helicopters, most prop aircraft, the corporate jet, and able to function as a Team member on the ground if needed.

Having finished reviewing the Team Mac and JC moved onto the House Team. Top Kiner, retired 1st Sergeant Marine Corps and resident Chief. Lady1 and LadyA, both former Intelligence Field Operatives, were very good at it, and one of the reasons they were selected. As for their code names, due to their completive natures and in order to maintain the sanity of both JJ and Mac who were issuing the code names, a compromise was agreed to and quickly finalized before one or both had a problem with being 'A' or '1.'

"JJ feels we should include Jar Head, Doggie, and Swabbie as part of the Team reviews. If we considered them as just special advisors, the Board would do it, but since they somehow managed to get themselves into the operational phase, JJ thought it best we do their reviews," Mac informed JC who agreed.

Jar Head, Doggie, and Swabbie were in retirement and had worked closely with Gil Dunn, Blue Jay and Bean during their years at the CIA.

They had joined the Team shortly after a foiled kidnapping and assassination attempt by Al-Qaida. The Agency knew about the Al-Qaida plot and were using the trio and their wives as bait, but had left them too exposed.

Di Flippi, a former associate and close friend still working at the CIA, notified Gil Dunn about the situation and since the Team was out of the country on a Project, the House Team traveled to Virginia, neutralized the Al-Qaida hit team, and then transported the trio and their wives back to a safe place in the area of the Barn where they would be protected. At first, Jar Head, Doggie, and Swabbie were unaware of the Team and the Board's activities, but it was just a matter of time before they sniffed out that something was going on and were asked to join the group. They had made big contributions during past Projects.

Having finished the process, Mac and JC decided a smoking break was in order. After both men had lit up cigars, Mac said, "Looking at the big picture, Al-Qaida has been quiet."

"Too quiet," JC quickly replied. "The U.S. drones seem to pop off a field leader every now and then, but the very high level players stay intact and that's where all major planning is done."

"Know what you're saying," Mac agreed. "How do you think Al-Qaida will function without Bin Laden?" he inquired.

"The same," JC replied. "Zawahiri, the supposed number two man, has always been the brains and planner. Bin Laden was more of a money man, but we can count on them making the most of his death to generate funds, recruitment, and to try something big against the U.S."

"Am afraid you're right," Mac agreed, shaking his head.

———

Top Kiner and the Ladies were in the kitchen having their morning coffee and enjoying a quiet moment prior to preparing the morning breakfast when a very loud and extended meow broke the silence, as Peeka entered the kitchen.

"Guess who's up?" Top said to the Ladies.

"And looking for breakfast," LadyA added.

"Are you hungry?' Lady1 inquired to Peeka and got a very soft, "Meow," in reply.

"Typical female, raise hell until they get what they want then get all soft and cuddly," Top said, as he stood and walked toward the pantry with Peeka trailing close behind. "Looks like we're all out of cat food," Top exclaimed, followed by a loud disagreeing report from Peeka, as both looked at the two stacks of canned cat food on the shelf. After a little more give and take, Top appeared with a can of Peeka's favorite cat food in hand explaining how he didn't see it, and Peeka responding with her usual long drawn out meow. This routine went on every morning with varying results, but it always gave Top and the Ladies a chuckle.

———————

When the Team was in residence at the Barn, three meals were prepared daily and served at the same times each day, also known as Chow Call. Today's breakfast menu consisted of oatmeal, scrambled eggs, bacon, sausage, home fried potatoes, toast, orange juice, and coffee, and the food was always arranged for self-service.

As the Team started to arrive from the Barn, Peeka, the Team's Mascot, greeted the men as they arrived and was petted by each.

It was about five minutes before the official Chow Call and all were waiting patiently for Top to give the go ahead before filling their plates. Then Air Jockey showed up and as usual, things changed.

"What's the hold up?" Jockey inquired.

"You're early," Top informed Jockey, knowing it wouldn't stop there.

"Early? My watch says breakfast is late," Jockey informed Top.

"The kitchen runs by my time," Top informed him, as he held up his left arm and pointed to his watch.

"More like you're running late because you got yourself confused again trying to follow one of Emeril's recipes. The way you screw up food, maybe we should change your name from Top to The Anti-Emeril."

"Along about now, I usually ask someone to pass me a big spoon," Top informed Jockey, "but not today. I'm going to try a different way to deal with you."

Jockey seemed puzzled at first, but then said, "I'm glad to hear you're finally realizing and accepting your place around here." He smiled and looked at the other Team Members. The smile was short lived as a big spoon smacked Jockey on the head.

"I thought you weren't going to do that anymore?" Jockey asked, as he rubbed his head.

"Said I was going to try a different way," Top corrected. "Instead of asking someone to pass me a big spoon, I'll just carry one with me," he informed Jockey, as he displayed a long heavy string that went around his neck then attached to the handle of a big spoon that hung alongside his leg.

JJ and Mac entered the kitchen and inquired about all of the laughter. When the Team members pointed toward Jockey and Top with the big spoon, JJ remarked, "Say no more," knowing what had probably happened.

"Maybe we should get his head checked?" Mac suggested.

"I don't think that spoon can do any damage," JJ replied.

"I mean a mental check," Mac corrected. "He keeps taunting Top about the food and always gets a big spoon to the head, but he wouldn't quit."

"I hear they weren't real big on mental checks where he got all of his flight training," JC announced. "Now what was the name of that outfit?" Faking a pause to think, he continued. "I know, it was Crotch Airways."

"So, we're going down that road again and before breakfast this time?" Jockey replied.

"Just making an observation," JC said with a smile.

"I'll attend to you later," Jockey informed Top who held up the big spoon in defense.

"So, again, you're saying my experience is not up to par with your Marine Corps background?" Jockey inquired to JC.

"Very good. Those hits to the head must be doing some good," JC replied.

"Could be," Jockey agreed. "Let me ask you something. Is it true the Marine Corps is really just the Navy's Army?" Jockey inquired, signaling the start of another humorous round of breakfast discussions.

After breakfast, JJ and Mac went back into the den to prepare for the following day's Board Meeting in New York City.

After covering what would be on the agenda, the two discussed something of a personal nature. Several of the Board members liked the area so much, that they decided to build country homes several miles from the Barn.

Since JJ had recommended people to Jar Head, Doggie, and Swabbie who had three homes built in the area in 2008, and were very pleased with the results, the Board members decided to use the same people for the construction of their houses.

Once again, with pencil in hand, JJ started a list. Carpenters—Steve (Farmer) Williamson & Associate Jake Stintsman, Dan Di Salvi's team, John Wicks and Tony Denise & his crew. Roofing—Joe Altvater and his four sons. Plumbing—Richard E. Yard's team and John Hoff & Associate. Heating & Cooling—Mark Vasey. Electrician— Karl Darby & Associate, Fred Nanni. Tile Contractor—Henry J. Piratzky. Painters—Dave Stryker and Michael Williams. Masons—Mitch Ege and team at Ege Masonry & Construction, Ben Andersen and Brian Slack & company. Excavation—George Kilmer, Jesse Lawson, and Roy Myers. Tree trimming and removal—Tom Karkas and his team from Northeast Tree Expert Company. Paving—Bob Brown & crew from R. M. Brown Company. Fuel oil—Stockton Fuel Oil and PFO. Appliances— Hendricks Appliances and Roger's Appliances. Home Insurance—Karen Thatcher.

Charles (Spooky) Rose and Tom Briggs would again be coaxed out of retirement along with Bobby Brown to add their expertise to the projects.

Always good work done by good people.

Chapter 2

Al-Qaida had moved its main operational center to Africa, but their operational planning for the attack on the Great Satan was located in Mexico. A house was rented in Mexico 10 miles from the U.S. border and for the past several years, had been used for meetings, planning, and now as a jumping off point for those crossing the border.

Since the Mexico/U.S. border was like a sieve and had been used many times in the past by Al-Qaida operatives, it would be no problem to use one of those same crossings. But since this was such a high priority mission, a different crossing was established where good fence security was backed up by miles of desert on the U.S. side and the reason people coming from Mexico didn't usually cross at that point.

During the first year after renting the house in Mexico, a tunnel was dug under the border to the U.S. side. In order not to reveal what they were doing, the work on the tunnel was only done during nighttime hours, the dirt from digging was dumped miles from the site, and all tire tracks were smoothed over to avoid detection from aircraft checking the border area.

Both ends of the tunnel weren't near any structures, concealed in plain sight, and since they were in one of the few locations where the fence and security was very good on the U.S. side, little attention was paid to the area, especially with no one attempting crossings.

The tunnel was used by operatives for control and communications to avoid the radio airways where things could be intercepted, but the primary reason for the elaborate tunnel was to ensure safe passage for what was to follow.

———

The Board meeting had covered financial matters and Mac had made his report on the Team reviews that he and JC had conducted.

With those items completed, JJ continued onto the next item. "Now for the Medical Support Area. Happy to say, Dr. D, MD, and Dr. C, MD, our Surgeon, are still onboard.

"As you all know, Check had completed two years of Medical School before making a career change and has continued to school Bris and Tic who are now at the Paramedic level. So, while on a Project, we have three Team Members for medical support.

"Our version of a Medivac-Jet, that now includes an upgraded operating theater, is still made ready and is positioned at a designated location when a Project is activated. The one thing we try to avoid is a Project on U.S. soil, but in that type of situation, the Medivac-Jet would fly the wounded out of the country. If the doctors advise against it, a hospital on U.S. soil would be used and we would deal with any fallouts about how the wounds were received later.

"Due to skill and a little luck, we have not required Medical Support in the past and let's all pray it stays that way."

Since they had been in session for over two hours, JJ thought it was time for a break. "Coffee anyone?"

Everyone was in agreement and headed to the back of the room to retrieve a much-needed cup of coffee.

After getting their coffee and after the conversations started to cycle down, JJ called the meeting back to order. "Before we move onto considering the list of Projects, do any of you have any questions, concerns or anything you would like to share?"

"Yes, Jeff?" JJ acknowledged Jeff Dawson who had motioned he had something to offer.

"Am still running that Oil Intel Network to keep track of what really is and isn't happening in the oil industry and as you all know from past Projects, things other than Oil Intel sometimes come my way. I would have submitted this for consideration as a Project, but I only found out about it prior to this meeting," Dawson started.

"I have unconfirmed Intel that Al-Qaida operatives are using the U.S./Mexico border to enter and leave for unknown reasons.

"I realize this is no big revelation since certain parts of the border are a complete joke in terms of security. They're used by anyone who wants to enter the country and is an ideal situation for a lone terrorist or groups of terrorists. What makes this interesting is the areas where it is so easy to cross are not being used, but rather an area where crossing is usually not attempted due to tighter security plus other reasons. If Al-Qaida has chosen a more difficult crossing and if there are no reports on file about sightings or apprehensions, the Intel reports are either wrong or the terrorists are being very careful. If the latter is the case, it can't be good," Dawson concluded.

"Is this coming from a reliable source within your Oil Intel Network?" Dunn inquired.

"The Intel is from the same source that made us aware of certain situations in the past that prompted us to mount successful Projects," Dawson replied.

After a great deal of discussion, JJ took the floor and called the meeting back to order. "Correct me if I'm wrong, but after listening to your opinions, it would seem a Project strictly for Intel gathering is in order?" All including Dawson were in total agreement.

"We'll take a vote, but it looks like Dawson has given us our next Project, especially since Al-Qaida may be involved," JJ continued.

After a vote was taken, the meeting continued. "I guess our next item on our agenda is the best way to proceed?" JJ offered.

After more discussion, the Board, per SOP, developed a high-level plan that JJ and General

Mac would present to the Team for discussion, recommendations, and approval. If accepted by the Team, a very detailed plan would be developed by JC and the Team. Since each Team Member had such a high level of expertise, this same procedure had been used since the Board and Team's inception and all Projects had been completed successfully.

With the planning completed, JJ ended the meeting with, "Hopefully, the Intel gathering Project will show the Intel was wrong, but if it is correct, we should be fully prepared to take some sort of action if required. The Teams are always prepared, so that leaves the logistics on our part."

The Board agreed and went into planning mode, the same way they did before each Project.

———————

The following morning, the Teams were assembled in the Team meeting room in the Barn and JJ had just completed the What part of the Project, and Mac was now at the pedestal to present the high-level How part.

"Morning, men," Mac started, and the Team replied.

"As JJ said, this will be an Intel gathering Project if you accept it. Per SOP, I will now present the Board's thoughts on how we might proceed. We all know the drill for something like this. The Intel may be bad, but if it is good, and Al-Qaida is in fact going to such great lengths to cross the border very quietly, the Board feels it can't be for anything good, so here are our thoughts.

"The area in question is along the el Centro, California sector of the U.S. border. The Team will form two groups, one for the Mexico side and the other for the U.S. side of the border.

"The Mexico Group will cross the border and set up in the area reported in the Intel. If people do appear, they will be kept under surveillance in an effort to discover the tunnel if one does exist. The group on the U.S. side will do the same.

"If either Group is forced into a confrontation, you will eliminate the Al-Qaida operatives, collect any Intel, and bury the bodies so they will not be discovered. Doing so would give more time for analysis while the Al-Qaida hierarchy tries to figure out what happened to their operatives since nothing had appeared in the media. Hopefully, you will not be forced into any confrontation and it will remain an Intel gathering Project, but we all know how quickly that can change, so extreme care should be taken.

"I'll now open it up to questions and/or comments," Mac informed the Teams.

"How long of an area along the border are we talking about?" JC inquired.

"We have narrowed it down to three miles," Mac answered.

"Since the Intel is very sketchy, I'm guessing nothing was reported about tunnel security being around the clock or just manned during the time of the crossings?" Blue Jay inquired.

"The Intel mainly covered the fact that Al-Qaida was making crossings in an area where border security was high opposed to the using one of the many areas where easy crossings are done every day," Mac replied.

"Three miles to cover with five on one side of the border and six on the other isn't a good idea," JC again spoke. "Maybe after analyzing the three-mile area, we will be able to narrow it down to the most likely area where a tunnel crossing would be taking place, and then we'll move onto a second phase."

"Around this point during past presentations, Mac and I usually leave, then return after the Team has discussed and voted on the Project. Are we at that point?" JJ inquired.

"In the interest of time and the fact that it is an Intel gathering Project, we can probably take a vote now. If it is yes and you have documentation about the border area in question, we can start planning right now," JC offered.

A vote was taken and the Team was in total agreement about accepting the Project. Now, the first phase planning started.

"The first thing we're changing is Intel gathering Project to Recon Project," JC informed everyone.

It was then decided in order to prove or disprove the location of a tunnel crossing surveillance sites would be first set up on the U.S. side of the border. If no sightings were made, the surveillance site would be adjusted.

Taking into consideration the possibility of a tunnel being manned 24/7, the surveillance sites would be established well back from the border area to avoid being caught between the border in front and a possible entrance behind.

The Team analyzed photos and maps of the border area in question that Mac and JJ had supplied, and after a few hours, all agreed on a point where initial surveillance would start and extend a little over half a mile to the east and west from that point.

Team members would be positioned every 400 feet on the U.S. side starting with Bean on the far left then Lady1, LadyA, Top Kiner, Benz, and Panda. Blue Jay would cover the center position with Bris, Tic, Check, and Air Jockey to his right.

Pru and Met would be 500 yards to the rear of the Teams and would be responsible for security/surveillance at the Teams' rear. The distance between them and all Team members would be well within their range and if necessary, they could terminate any aggressive action taken against any Team member.

With initial phase planning completed, JC inquired, "Any questions or comments?" With none, he ended the planning session.

Chapter 3

Since border crossings would probably not be attempted during daylight hours, the Teams were deployed after dark each night, and then would depart each morning when the night sky started giving a hint it was going to give way to daylight.

To avoid making anyone curious or possibly alerting any terrorists in the area during daylight hours, the Teams were staying at a remote house 15 miles from the site and for the past nine days, were transported to and from the area using two vans driven by JC and Mac.

Upon arrival, the Teams would prepare for that night's activities, then after dark would very quietly move into their positions covering their tracks as they moved so as not to leave footprints that could be detected. Once the Teams were underway, Mac and JC would depart the area so they wouldn't attract any attention.

The following morning after the order was heard over their com headsets, they would depart the same way they arrived, and then were picked up by the vans at a different location.

It was late afternoon of the tenth day and a meeting was called to evaluate the situation. JC had just taped a large map to the wall and then started with, "We have had nine nights of super quiet and the question now is should we move to the east or west to cover another area?" After the Teams discussed the what-ifs and other items, JC again took the floor and said, "We'll keep these positions for a few more nights and then relocate."

It was another very quiet night on the border when Bean's voice was heard over everyone's com headset. "Activity at the left flank on the Mexico side about two hundred yards out."

"How many?" Blue Jay inquired.

"I count eight. The two in front and two at the rear are carrying what looks like automatic weapons. The other four have backpacks, not sure about what arms they're carrying," Bean answered.

"Sounds like a drug shipment to me," Blue Jay replied.

"That would be my guess," Bean agreed.

"We'll stay in quiet mode and let them pass through," Blue Jay advised everyone.

Everyone was watching every move the eight made as they approached the border fence when Pru whispered, "I say, there seems to be some activity at our rear."

Since Pru and Met were 500 yards back from the border, it was either the Border Patrol, police or some bad guys meeting up with this other group, Blue Jay thought. "Are you in a bad position?" Blue Jay inquired.

"Not at the present," Pru answered. "They're approximately fifty yards to our right heading toward the fence."

"Keep the most heavily armed in your scopes in case they are bad guys and shit happens," Blue Jay instructed.

"Did you people to the right copy that?" Blue Jay asked, making sure they received the communications from Pru.

To hold down on communications, the Team members replied to Blue Jay with a series of clicks when possible. To the right, it started with one and ended with four. When Blue Jay heard all of the clicks, he knew they had all received the communications.

Since Tic was the Spanish speaker on the Team, in addition to night vision gear, he had a listening device that could pick up conversations at long range and was zeroed in on the group approaching from the Mexico side of the border.

"Check, I'm picking up some strange shit here," Tic whispered into his com unit. "Instead of just hearing Spanish, I'm hearing Spanish and what sounds like Arabic."

"Let's have a listen," Check replied, and Tic put his com unit next to the listening device receiver. There was complete silence for a minute or so, but as the group got closer, they started talking again.

When the talking stopped, Tic inquired, "Could you hear that?"

"Yes and it's Arabic," Check confirmed.

What the hell is going on, drug smuggling or terrorism?

Blue Jay thought. After some additional thought, he said, "Let's see how this plays out. Tic, you and Check see if you can pick up any conversation that will tell us what these people are really up to."

The group approaching from the U.S. side had passed wide to the right of the Team's position and was at the border fence. All communications at the fence was in Spanish prior to four backpacks being catapulted over the 18-foot high border fence. That completed, the two groups went their separate ways, but the group on the U.S. side were not taking the same route and were instead, heading straight for the middle the Team's positions.

"Stay cool in the pool, people," Blue Jay instructed, knowing the percentages were on the Team's side.

Since they were walking in single file and with over 130 yards between each Team member, the drug smugglers should pass between them, but sometimes shit happens.

It wasn't long before they saw the back of the last man and if they maintained that course, the group would pass wide to the left of Pru and Met. But suddenly, they changed to a course that would take them very close to Pru and Met.

Realizing this, Blue Jay was on the com. "Bean, move everyone in close and watch those other turds in Mexico. If anything happens, engage them if they attempt to come over the fence."

"Roger that," Bean replied, already on the move.

"Bris, Tic, Jockey, you're with me. We're moving back toward Pru and Met's position. Check, you join up with Bean in case those Arab speakers return." Nothing else had to be said, everyone knew what to do and why.

The drug runners didn't seem to be concerned about being quiet during their return and could be heard talking at quite a distance. "Can you hear what they're saying?" Blue Jay asked Tic.

"They're bitching about why they have to come out here to get the drugs," Tic replied, then said, "Wait one," as he listened to additional chatter. "That was an interesting bit," Tic continued. "The leader told them the Arabs agreement was to escort and protect the drugs through Mexico, but they wouldn't enter the U.S."

Blue Jay and the other three were quickly closing the gap as the group approached their Teammate's position. The drug runners were almost past when the fourth man carrying a backpack lost his balance and fell into Pru and Met's position and almost immediately, two of the men with weapons at the ready were looking down at the duo before they could react. Pru and Met had their 9mm Berettas in hand, but were hampered by the man who had fallen on top of them. The two drug runners took aim, then muffled gunfire was heard.

Knowing that sound very well, Blue Jay and the others rushed to the area, but it was all over before they got there.

As Blue Jay and the others entered the scene from different angles, they were surprised to see four men standing over dead bodies. Noticing their surprise, JC announced, "I guess these children thought we were going to leave them out here all by themselves."

"Imagine that," Mac replied, as he checked out one of the backpacks.

"Bean, is the group in Mexico still moving away?" Blue Jay inquired into his com unit.

"No problem," he replied. "We didn't hear anything, so I'm sure they didn't. Wonder if anyone else did?"

"What made you think something was going to happen tonight?" Blue Jay asked JC.

"It's Mac. He has been eating gypsy shit again," JC replied.

"Yeah, that plus there wasn't anything good on TV tonight and we wanted something to do," Mac added.

"So, they've been babysitting us every night?" Jockey guessed.

"Somebody has to," Mac remarked, as he checked one of the dead men for ID.

"Are you hearing this, Panda?" Jockey inquired over the com.

"Yeah," Panda answered. "It's all part of that gung ho Marine Corps bullshit, like holding a bayonet between your teeth and charging a machine gun nest."

JC and Mac chuckled at Panda's reply and would continue that discussion at a later date.

"There's a shitload of what may be cocaine in these backpacks," JC informed the others, as he removed a packet and displayed it.

"Call in the Teams," JC instructed. "We better get moving in case someone is waiting and comes looking for these people."

Blue Jay advised the Teams to join him. He also told Bean and Check to drop off on the way back and serve as a listening post in case more than drug runners or someone else was in the area.

After the Teams were assembled, the six bodies were moved a few hundred yards to the west, and then buried with empty backpacks. If the bodies were discovered, it would look like the work of what law enforcement were calling rip teams, or drug dealers that rip off other drug dealers.

With that completed, the Teams moved another 50 yards to the west, dug another hole, cut open each packet, emptied the contents into the hole, then threw in the empty bags. After the last bag was emptied, the hole was filled in.

When that was completed, Blue Jay inquired, "Any type of activity at the listening post?"

Bean quickly replied, "Negative," and was instructed to join the others.

When Bean and Check arrived, the others were ready to travel, and since the pickup point had changed, due to JC and Mac being with the Teams, they took the lead to where they had stashed the vans. Moving very quickly, they arrived at their destination just as the first sign of light was in the morning sky. After the Teams performed a security check of the area, they loaded up and were underway.

There would be many discussions during the trip back and at the safe house: Were they compromised by their activities? They were planning to move to another area, but if they were compromised, would it just be a waste of time? What about those Arab speaking people guarding the drugs? Are they active terrorists or just terrorists generating money for their cause?

Later that morning, it was decided that the Arab speaking people guarding the drug situation would be kicked up to the Board and the Teams would focus on the primary objective. By mid-afternoon, the Teams were still engaged in full-time discussions.

"Let's take it from the top again," JC suggested. "If we were compromised last night by terrorists who are crossing the border, it probably means we were at the right place and the Intel is good, but they now know we were there. On the other hand, if we were not compromised last night, it could mean we were in the wrong place or the terrorists have not been crossing or the Intel is no good."

It was late in the afternoon when JC and Mac realized the Teams had been at it too long. "So, what is your professional opinion, General Mac?" JC inquired.

"I'd rather not say," Mac answered. "I'm fresh out of gypsy shit. There are some good shows on TV tonight and I'm in no mood for babysitting."

The Teams were feeling numb from all of the talking and were very slow to respond, until Jockey said, "Gung Ho Fuck," then all hell broke loose.

Can always depend on Mac to help motivate the troops, JC thought.

After the humorous verbal brawl subsided, the Teams took a break for refreshments.

When the meeting reconvened an hour later, JC announced, "Due to the previous night's activities, the Teams will be standing down tonight. We don't want a firefight with drug dealers who are out there looking for their drugs. Plus, if terrorists are in the area, they may have seen all of the activity last night as just drug-related and we don't want to change that. So, everyone rest up for round two," he suggested.

Chapter 4

Around 11:00 P.M. that night, four figures on the Mexico side of the border moved very cautiously, as they approached the area where the drug exchange took place the previous night. The four went into a kneeling position and were checking out the area very thoroughly.

"Can someone tell me what we're doing in Mexico without support?" Bean inquired over the com.

"Welcome to a Marine Corps Fire Team recon patrol," JC replied.

"More like Huey, Dewey, and Louie out for a walk with Uncle Donald," Blue Jay observed.

"If you ladies are done complaining, we'll move to the east and continue the search," JC said into the com.

The four had made a wide circle and approached the area using the same route the drug runners had the night before. If they were under observation, hopefully, they would be taken for drug runners. To help with the deception, Blue Jay and Bean were carrying backpacks and Donald and Huey put on a little act now and then trying to give the impression that they were lost.

The four men had almost reached the end of their east search grid when Tic alerted the others of movement at their two o'clock. The four men very slowly went into a kneeling position and while JC tried to ID the movement, the others focused to the right, left, and rear of their position to avoid any unpleasant surprises.

"Looks like ten men. Don't see any backpacks, so they may not be runners," JC whispered into his com unit. "Let's get low and watch these turds."

All four men went into the phone position, still maintaining their 360-degree surveillance.

"They definitely know where they're going," JC informed the others. "Question being, is it the border fence or did we get lucky?"

JC's recon patrol followed the 10 men at very long range so they wouldn't alert them and only moved when the 10 men were almost out of sight. This was a good strategy until the 10 men disappeared.

"Well, that worked out well. They didn't reach the fence, but they're gone," JC said into the com, as he checked the GPS for their location. "We'll wait a while to see if they pop up somewhere else."

After an hour of watching with no movement whatsoever, the four men departed, first at a crawl, then walking low and slow. When they reached the point where they had started the surveillance, they continued for approximately two miles then headed toward the border.

When Huey, Dewey, Louie, and Uncle Donald were getting close to the border, Louie said, "So that was a Marine Corps Fire Team recon patrol?"

"Yeah," Dewey answered. "Wasn't it exciting?"

"Now we have to hope Uncle Donald doesn't fuck up and get us caught by the U.S. border patrol," Huey added.

"Knew I should have brought Mac instead of you people," JC defended. "He appreciates Marine Corps tactics and doesn't complain nearly as much as you Hairy Marys."

When the four reached the fence, they catapulted the backpacks over the same way they saw the drug runners do it, then two at a time they scaled the fence.

When all four were again on U.S. soil, JC stood looking at the fence for a moment. "Hardly seems worth the money. If you three Marys can climb over it, anyone can." Then he turned and proceeded to where they had left their vehicle.

Huey, Dewey, and Louie chuckled as they followed, knowing they had pissed off Uncle Donald.

When the four men returned to the house, it was in the A.M. hours and after briefing the Teams about what they had found, everyone turned in for some much-needed sleep.

At the daily meeting, JC went into greater detail about the recon patrol, presented his thoughts, and new plans for that night's activities. "Since we made a wide sweep into Mexico, then approached the area using a route we know was used by drug runners, hopefully we gave the impression that we were also drug runners and were no threat to any terrorists in the area. If other drug people observed us and since we don't plan to go into Mexico again anytime soon, that shouldn't be a problem. However, we should be more alert for activity on the U.S. side of the border. We'll be positioned one and one half miles east from our last location, but drug runners may be in the area trying to find their missing shipment, so maybe we should close it up a little?"

At that point, JC opened up the meeting and it was decided to shorten the distance from 400 to 200 feet between Team members, bringing the long-range shooters in from 500 to 250 yards.

Additional items were addressed, then Jockey inquired, "Will JC and Mac be in the area tonight or is there something good on TV?"

Before JC or Mac could respond, Blue Jay added, "You can bet Uncle Donald will be out there tonight."

"Uncle Donald?" Jockey inquired.

"Yeah, we didn't tell you about that part of the Recon patrol yet," Bean advised.

"Oh, good, new material," Jockey said while rubbing his hands together.

Mac looked at JC with a questioning look and he said, "It's a long story."

Mac knew that somehow, he would be on the receiving end of the Uncle Donald humor and the thought was still in his head when he heard, "It seems unfair that JC is Uncle Donald and General Mac is just plain Mac," Jockey stated, as he looked in Panda's direction.

"How about Phineas Mac Duck?" Panda offered.

"Good one," Jockey approved, already knowing Panda would come up with something.

"Like I don't already have enough problems, Uncle Donald!" Mac advised JC, as both men smiled and shook their heads.

The Teams had been at their new position for three nights with nothing to report. It looked like the fourth night was going to have the same results until Blue Jay was on the com. "Bean, Tic, do some of those turds approaching from the Mexico side look familiar?" he inquired.

"Yep," both men replied.

"Let's see where they disappeared to the other night," Blue Jay added.

All eyes were on the 10 men as they approached the border then disappeared from view for Blue Jay and everyone to his right. "Lost visual," Blue Jay informed the others.

"Have entrance," Bean replied from the far left of their recon line. "Three small knolls about one hundred fifty feet from fence. Entrance must be in the center knoll."

With that information, Blue Jay was again on the com. "If they dug in a straight line, the entrance on this side should be somewhere between Benz and Panda, so let's give them a wide passage."

No other instructions had to be given as Benz and Panda doubled the space between their positions.

The Teams had held their positions for three hours without any activity occurring on the U.S. side of the border when a portion of the sand between Benz and Panda's positions started to rise up and then stopped approximately four feet in the air.

Blue Jay was immediately on the com. "These people are using what looks like a sandbox type entrance, approximately four feet square, probably operated with some sort of hydraulic lift. Am sure the primary people making the crossing will continue with some sort of security escort, so stay alert. Bean, Jockey, since you are both on the extreme flanks, you'll maintain parallel surveillance of whoever comes out from under the sandbox. The remainder will wait until everything quiets down, then Lady1, LadyA, Top Kiner, Benz, and Panda will move to the left flank and follow Bean's route. Bris, Tic, Check, and I will go to the right and follow Jockey's route. That will leave the center open if the escorts make a return trip to the sandbox."

Blue Jay was still on the com when the first head popped out of the hole. He surveyed the area, then quickly moved to a position a short distance away, and again, surveyed the area. After he was satisfied it was clear, he motioned for the others to follow, and one by one, seven men quickly joined him. After the eighth man was out, the sandbox slowly lowered until the desert was again flat.

"Eight men, not ten are continuing on," Blue Jay alerted everyone over the com. "These turds look like they've done this before, so don't crowd them."

The sandbox was a good name for the entrance to the tunnel. How better to create a concealed opening in the desert? A reinforced non-metallic box with sand colored sides, four inches high, and one quarter inch thick, operated by a hydraulic system. With the box filled with sand, it's invisible in the desert and to metal detectors.

Bean and Jockey had both moved in closer, but just close enough to keep the group in sight, as they moved due north through the desert.

Two hours later, Bean and Jockey still had the eight under surveillance with the remainder of the teams within striking distance if Bean or Jockey were discovered and required assistance.

"They've stopped for a break or have reached their rendezvous point," Bean informed everyone over the com.

"Maybe they put in a subway line, too, and are just waiting for a train," Jockey offered.

"At ease, Crotch Airways," JC's voice came over the com.

"Is that you, Uncle Donald?" Jockey inquired. "Is Phineas with you or is there something good on TV tonight?"

JC didn't reply; he just looked at Mac. Both smiled and again shook their heads.

After a 30 minute wait, the sound motors in the distance could be heard.

"Sounds like somebody's ride is about to arrive," Bean commented.

After a brief wait, two dune buggies appeared in the distance and headed in the direction of the eight men. Since they were also using GPS devices, there was little chance for error when making a pickup.

When the two dune buggies stopped next to the group of men, one of them carrying a backpack climbed in and after a brief discussion, the dune buggies made a 180 degree turn and sped off.

"Bean, Jockey, keep them in sight as long as possible," Blue Jay instructed. "We'll make sure the others clear the area."

"And I left my sneakers back at the ranch," Jockey complained, as he moved quickly to observe the two buggies.

With their escort duty completed, the seven men started moving back toward the border.

When Blue Jay was satisfied they had left the area and were in fact heading back to the sandbox, he ordered, "Move out," over the com.

Blue Jay and the others would have a lot of questions at their next Team meeting. Why use this place to cross when in other areas, they could have just walked across the border to catch their ride? Why such an elaborate entrance? Why so much security? Defending against drug runners and rip teams possibly, but why the second dune buggy with heavily armed men?

Many questions to be answered prior to planning phase two of the Project.

———————

Since phase two would be very demanding considering the total size of the Teams, they moved back to the Barn to conduct planning.

JJ and the Board had been kept informed on a daily basis and were already up to speed when JJ called the Board meeting to order the day after General Mac and the Teams returned.

"First, I want to thank Dawson and his Oil Intel for making us aware of what looks like a very sophisticated operation on the U.S./Mexico border. It's obvious if someone put that much effort into the crossing, it has to be for something very big, but what?"

"Mac, we've been conducting meetings in your absence. Have come up with how we would like to proceed, but have waited for your return and your input." JJ continued. "We went over this problem from every angle, but feel with the amount of manpower at our disposal, we cannot continue with this Project. The Board members again volunteered their services and we still came up short."

"May I add the Board will be meeting at a later date to discuss how the members seem to be getting a little too eager to get involved in Projects these days."

"It's our bucks and our asses," Wilson spoke up.

"Get 'em, Weed Whacker," Mac encouraged.

"Like I said, we'll have a meeting at a later date," JJ reaffirmed, then continued. "Bottom line is, we feel it's best to funnel it to the federal government who have the manpower and resources to continue."

"Have to agree," Mac said. "JC and I have come up with the same conclusion; however, the Teams may not agree. They don't like to give up on anything, especially if they're already in the middle."

"We'll explain to them at tomorrow's meeting," JJ replied, then inquired, "Then we're all agreed?" and the Board members shook their heads to confirm.

"Well, Gil, I guess it's now up to you to get it to the federal people?"

"Already have a meeting planned for tomorrow," Gil Dunn assured JJ who called the meeting to a close.

———

Late spring at the Gettysburg Battlefield was very pleasant. The results from more than usual spring rainfall made everything bloom to its max and was surrounded with beautiful shades of green.

There was a part of the battlefield that wasn't visited that much due to it being off the beaten path at the park. It was where the cavalry from north and south had their great clash during the Battle at Gettysburg. General Lee instructed Jeb Stuart to circle around and attack the Union lines from the rear, but Brigadier Generals Gregg and Custer intercepted Stuart and the battle was on with move and then counter move. The cavalry battle was considered a draw, but since Jeb Stuart was unable to attack the Union lines from the rear, it contributed to the South losing at Gettysburg that third day.

Gil was already at the meeting place looking out over the flat fields where some of the cavalry battle took place when

Di Flippi arrived. "What's wrong with this picture?" Di said. "I'm usually the one waiting for you."

Without a pause, Dunn replied, "Askers arrive first."

"So, you're saying I'm usually asking for something?" Di inquired with a smile.

"Well, yeah," Dunn replied.

"Get stuffed," Di answered, as he handed Dunn a Cuban cigar.

"Are these still illegal in this country?" Dunn inquired.

"They were illegal all of the other times I gave you one and nothing's changed."

"Just checking," Dunn replied, as he took the cigar.

After lighting up their cigars and taking a few puffs, Di Flippi said, "I'm thinking about this cavalry battle and the generals who participated. One in particular was considered the hero of the battle, was promoted to Major General a year later, got screwed after the war, was reduced to Lieutenant Colonel, and then Custer had some unpleasantness with the Indians. So, are you trying to tell me what you're asking for may lead to a bunch of politicians running around in circles demanding my scalp?"

"Now you're confusing what I want with the shit you usually ask me for. This one is simple and if you don't screw it up, you may even get some parse."

"Okay, okay, the suspense is killing me. What is it?" Di inquired and then faked a yawn.

"Oh, that's clever, is that new?" Dunn asked, commenting on the yawning. "Anyway, here's the poop," he continued.

When Dunn had finished, Di told him how he would go about relaying the information to the FBI. "Think the best way to go about this would be my people got a tip about something else, were on the Mexico side of the border, and observed the crossing, but I'll leave out the dune buggy part. Since two of my people were sort of in on that island thing, thought I would use them. Do you remember the Seal and Major Tex?"

"I do," Dunn confirmed. "Think they would be open to any offers outside the Agency?"

"Not so fast," Di cut him off. "You don't recruit them for whatever it is you're doing until after I retire."

"Still trying to claim innocence?" Dunn observed. "I don't think, 'No, your honor, I didn't know what Dunn was up to,' will work."

"Yes, it will," Di assured him. "That plus a dumb look on my face should get me off with only life in the big house."

After the duo had a chuckle, Di got serious. "Sounds like bad shit brewing."

"I agree," Dunn said. "It's very obvious that if a terrorist organization puts that many resources into just making border crossings, it's something really big."

"But will those political types at Justice think it is?" Di questioned.

Dunn was silent for a while, and then said, "If we were dealing with the FBI office in New York City or even a field office, I'd say we'd have no problems, but FBI HQ in Washington? Maybe we should pick our next meeting place concerning this topic now just in case? How do you feel about the peach orchard?"

"What better place?" Di replied. "If we have to meet about this again, I'm sure by that time, everything will be just peachy."

Chapter 5

JJ had already informed the Teams he would like to speak with them after breakfast, so when JJ and Mac entered the Team meeting room, all were in attendance.

The two men walked to the front of the room and JJ started the meeting with, "We have two items to cover this morning. First, the Board and I would like to again commend all of you for an excellent job. Know I have said that many times, but today, it's no less sincere than the first time."

"Don't like where this is going," Jockey whispered to Panda who just smiled.

"As for phase two of the Project, we have decided, due to our size, it would be best to channel your findings to the FBI. I realize this is a first, but we feel keeping surveillance while trying not to alert the individuals would be too risky. Are there any questions or comments?" JJ asked the Teams.

"We came to the same conclusion," JC spoke up. "No matter how many ways we ran it, we always came up with the same conclusion, not enough recourses."

"I'm glad we all agree," JJ said, relieved the Teams were in agreement with the Board.

"The second item is," JJ continued, "the Board would appreciate it if you all would not take leave at this time."

Since the normal mode of operation for the Team was to take leave after a Project this request was unusual and probably for a good reason so the Team went along with the request, eventually.

The Team started buzzing about what JJ had asked when Jockey inquired, "I usually get a kiss after sex. Will we all be getting a kiss?"

After a few more one-liners, JJ got the Teams settled down and said, "You've caught me off guard. I thought the first item would have gotten this kind of reaction."

Blue Jay then spoke up. "Is there another important Project that may be coming our way?"

"There's nothing definite yet, but when some of the Intel you people gathered is combined with Intel from other sources, it could add up to another Project," JJ replied.

That said, the Teams quieted down until LadyA announced, "You'll love it hanging around the house and Barn like we do when you're all away at those exotic places enjoying yourselves."

"Boohoo, what a bunch of sissies," Lady1 added, not wanting to let a good opportunity go to waste. "Cheer up, you'll like it. We even rent cows for morning milking to help keep up our covert cover."

Since the Team members were never at a loss for words, someone said, "Milk this."

"This isn't good," Mac informed JJ.

"No, shit," he replied, as the back and forth continued.

When things finally started to calm down, Mac inquired, "Bean, Blue Jay, can't you keep your women under control?"

JJ looked at Mac who replied, "I was feeling left out."

"Their women?" the Ladies exploded.

"Our women?" Bean and Blue Jay exploded.

"I think it's time to leave," Mac advised.

"And quickly," JJ added.

Having made it out of the Barn without being stoned, the two were walking back to the house when JJ said, "Can't you keep your women under control? You missed your calling; you are definitely diplomatic material. Getting you a position at the UN might help the world situation."

"If I went to the UN, who would keep track of the Board's financial investments during a Project? Like, why were all of those expensive weapons given to freedom fighters like Charley Tuna in Cuba?"

"Don't start with that shit again," JJ advised, repeating, "Charley Tuna."

"How about Sunny Sands over in the Middle East?" Mac kept on talking.

With that, JJ turned around and headed back to the Barn. "I'd rather run the chance of being stoned than listen to that bullshit again."

"So, you're saying you don't remember Sunny?" Mac continued, causing JJ to throw his hands in the air and walk faster.

If Mac would just explain to JJ the situations and why the weapons had to be disposed of, there would be no problem, but there was no fun in that, so instead of explaining things like, The Team had to dismantle the weapons and dump them into the sea in case they were stopped, Mac told JJ, "We gave the weapons to Charley Tuna, that Cuban freedom fighter." Of course, each freedom fighter had their own story that became more unbelievable with each Project and JJ would always try to maintain his cool, but Mac would keep going until he finally lost control.

———

To help the Team deal with the downtime while at the Barn, the next morning at breakfast, JJ shared a list of some restaurants in the area. As the Team members reviewed the list, they asked about the cuisine at Lambertville Station, Stockton Inn, De Anna's, INN of the Hawk, Giuseppe's Pizza & Family Restaurant and others on the list. Both JJ and Mac answered their questions since they had frequented all of them during the time they were in the planning stages of how to establish the Board and Teams.

"I just ask one thing," JJ requested. "Don't all pile into one of these places at the same time. We're talking small towns here and in a small town, word travels fast."

"What should be the max number, two, four?" Mac inquired.

"I would suggest four at the maximum," JJ replied.

"That's good," Mac shook his head in approval. "That means Blue Jay, Bean, and the Ladies can double date."

Everyone braced for the explosion that was about to come when Lady1 said, "That would be delightful."

"Yes, since we all have been so busy, we haven't had an opportunity to enjoy a lovely night of dining," LadyA added.

Everyone looked at Bean and Blue Jay who were quick to say, "What kind of cuisine do you prefer?" and "Do you prefer cuisine over ambiance?"

The stunned members at the table just looked at each other for a few seconds and then Panda inquired, "Is this some sort of brainwashing experiment or something? Cancel a Project in the middle, cancel our leave, now this."

"It's already melting my melon," Jockey added.

"Whatever do you mean?" Lady1 asked in a soft, inquiring voice.

"Maybe they flipped out and we all should make a run for it," Panda offered.

"Don't listen to these Cro-Magnons," Bean told the Ladies, as he and Blue Jay stood up and asked, "How about dining tonight."

"You pick the place and we'll pick you up around eight," Blue Jay added.

The four continued their conversation as they left a room full of stunned men.

"Now see what you've done?" JJ confronted Mac. "Like I don't have enough to worry about.

They may be busting our balls, but what if it develops into something more? Stranger things have happened."

Mac just sat quietly, then JJ inquired, "Well, don't you have anything to say?"

"Yes, I do," Mac replied. "Are you sure you don't remember Charley Tuna?"

It wasn't the explosion the Team thought they were going to experience earlier, but JJ was a close second, as he went bullshit on Mac.

That evening at the house while LadyA and Lady1 were getting ready to go out, JJ was looking out one of the windows in his den when he saw Bean and Blue Jay get out of their car. The Team members always used the kitchen door when arriving or departing, but this time, the duo went toward the front door of the house.

Two can play that game, JJ thought, as he quickly left the den.

After knocking on the front door, Blue Jay and Bean were surprised to see JJ, Mac, and Top Kiner standing there, as the door swung open.

"Come in," JJ invited, as Lady1 and LadyA entered the room.

"Is this a reception committee?" Bean inquired.

"Sort of," JJ replied seriously. "We want to know what your intentions are."

At that point, General Mac addressed the two as if he were giving a briefing at the Pentagon.

"Since the young women are living here away from home, we feel responsible and are acting as their surrogate fathers."

The duo were caught off guard, but quickly recovered with, "Sir, I assure you this is just an evening of dining," Blue Jay said.

Seeing what was happening, the Ladies quickly came to their rescue and ushered the duo out the front door.

"Don't be out too late, remember your curfew," JJ ordered.

"And don't you guys get handsie with the Ladies either," Top Kiner instructed for the final touch.

As JJ closed the door, he remarked, "That went rather well for such short notice."

"Don't get handsie was a nice touch," Mac told Top.

"Wonder what we could have come up with if we had more notice?" JJ said, as he guided the other two men toward his den and a few brew.

"What are they really up to?" Mac wondered aloud then added, "What do you think, Peeka?"

Peeka, never being short on replies, let out a long drawn out Meow, as she followed them to the den.

"She seems to have strong feelings about it," Mac commented.

"Either that or she wants something to eat," Top replied, as Peeka looked up at him and gave a soft meow.

"I'll get her something," Mac volunteered, then both headed for the kitchen. "For as much as you eat, I'm beginning to wonder if you're a mountain lion in cat's clothing. Speaking of mountain lions, remember that time you scared Uncle Blue Jay in the woods?" Mac said and Peeka let out a very long reply. When she stopped, Mac inquired, "So, you're saying Blue Jay is a sissy boy?"

"Well, I guess we have a heads up about Mac's next verbal attack on Blue Jay," JJ observed.

———

JJ told the Team to enjoy themselves, so they did and were out of booze within three days. Bean and Blue Jay volunteered to make a booze run and were waiting for the red light to change at the corner of Bridge and Main Street in Lambertville.

"What's wrong with this picture?" Bean asked. "Every other time we sat here at a red light looking at Cifelli's Sunoco, we were on a Project and en route to fly out of Mercer Airport."

"I was thinking the same thing when we passed the Lambertville Police Department Headquarters," Blue Jay replied. "Seems strange doesn't it?"

When the light changed to green, Blue Jay turned right and proceeded to Union Street two blocks away, then turned left, proceeded halfway down the block, and then parked. Blue Jay and Bean with lists in hand then proceeded across the street to the Wonderful World of Wines store to purchase the requested booze.

With help from the staff, the duo had gotten everything on the lists and was leaving the store each carrying a box of bottles, followed by two of the staff, each carrying a box of bottles as well.

"How are we going to fit all of this stuff into your Porsche?" Bean inquired.

"Very carefully," Blue Jay replied.

After finding room for all of the bottles and expressing their appreciation for the help, Bean and Blue Jay prepared for the trip back to the Barn.

Following Bean's directions, Blue Jay continued south to the end of Main Street, turned left onto Mount Hope, then made a quick right onto Wilson Street. "A trip down memory lane," Bean said, as they passed the YMAC, a private club. "This is where I came close to that nice lady getting out of a tan Chevy and she made a gesture at Benz and me."

"Did she?" Blue Jay inquired.

"Yep, and we chuckled about it on and off until we arrived at the airport," Bean answered.

After turning onto Feeder Street, Blue Jay paused at the stop sign.

"Notice you keep checking out the rearview mirror," Bean observed.

"The car behind us keeps making the same turns we do. Probably nothing," Blue Jay replied.

"Well, it can't be crazy again because you punched his ticket in Jamaica," Bean observed.

"Let's see what it does now," Blue Jay said, as he turned right onto Route 29 South.

The Porsche quickly passed the River Walk office complex, the Lace Works, and looked like it was going to leave the city limits, but then made a quick U-turn by Towel Towing. The Porsche continued on Route 29 North until it came to the traffic light at Bridge Street, made a left turn, then a quick right into an alley next to Walker's Wine & Spirits. After a few more turns the Porsche was on Route 179 North and proceeded up a long hill leading away from town. A few miles later, the car in question was still behind them. "Okay, let's see what's really going on," Blue Jay said, as he pulled into Amwell Automotive's front parking lot and stopped.

The car behind slowed down a little, but passed, and continued up the road.

Looks like a carload of youngsters to me, Bean observed, as the car in question pulled to the side of the road about a quarter of a mile further on.

Blue Jay made another U-turn onto 179 South and took off at high speed.

Observing this, the other car also made a U-turn.

"Looks like they want to play," Blue Jay observed.

The Porsche started down the long hill and when out of sight of the following car, Blue Jay pulled onto a side road, spun around so he was again pointing south, turned off the headlights, and waited.

"Are you going to harass these youngsters?" Bean inquired.

"A little," Blue Jay confirmed. "I noticed a Lambertville police officer sitting in a lot watching traffic when we came up the hill. If it's still there, maybe we came shake these youngsters up twice?"

As the trailing car passed where the duo were waiting, the Porche pulled onto the highway and up behind the car still with no lights on. When they were almost bumper-to-bumper, Blue Jay turned on the high beam headlights and laid on the horn while Bean hung out the window yelling and screeching.

At first, the driver was startled, but then he floored the gas pedal trying to get away. The car was doing 60 where the speed limit was 30 by the time they reached York Street. Blue Jay quickly hit the brakes and turned onto York while the other vehicle continued on and past the police officer who was sitting 100 yards away.

"Maybe they'll think twice next time before harassing two harmless people out making a booze run," Blue Jay commented.

———

Another three weeks had passed and the Team was still onsite at the Barn.

It was a beautiful morning. Mac had just gotten another cup of coffee and went out onto the deck at the side of the house to enjoy the nice weather when Top and the Ladies heard him remark, "Somebody's following Peeka home."

When Top and the Ladies went out onto the deck, Mac pointed toward the long lane that ran from the house to the road that passed by the house.

When they looked in the direction Mac was pointing, they saw a little puppy walking behind Peeka up the lane and every time the puppy fell too far behind, Peeka stopped or went back to the puppy.

"Looks more like Peeka is bringing somebody home," Top remarked.

"I'll bet someone dumped the poor thing off along the road," LadyA remarked.

"Well, that's how Peeka got here, so maybe she decided to adopt the puppy," Lady1 remarked.

It was a cute little puppy being a cross between a pug and a shepherd with the tan and black color and tail of a pug, but a little bigger than a pug with a shepherd's snout.

"We just can't turn it away or take it to the pound," LadyA expressed, concerned.

"I don't know how JJ would react to another animal in the house," Mac said.

"Maybe we can coax him into letting the puppy stay?" Lady1 wondered.

"We can try," Mac agreed, and the four started conspiring, as Peeka continued to usher the puppy toward the house.

After arriving at the deck, the puppy was a little afraid, but very friendly, as everyone greeted it. At the same time, they gave Peeka praise for her new adoption, and a lot of petting, as well as for the puppy.

While all of this was going on, JJ came out onto the deck with coffee cup in hand to see what all the commotion was about.

"Look what Peeka brought home," Lady1 said, activating the plan the four had agreed on.

"The puppy is so cute," LadyA continued.

"Yeah, yeah, so cute. We'll call it Sandy. Better ask the Team to get it some gear from PetsMart. They know the drill from when Peeka arrived," JJ replied, returning to his den.

"'We'll call it Sandy,' and 'the Team knows the drill,' he says, just as nice as you please," Mac remarked, and then said, "Well, Sandy it is," as he reached down to pet the puppy and another member was added to the Teams.

Sandy was a playful puppy and Peeka was still young enough to enjoy playing, so they would make good company for each other.

Chapter 6

After an additional two weeks of downtime at the Barn, JJ called a meeting to present another Project for the Teams' review.

Due to the additional Intel discovered during the recon Project, the Board kept the Team close while they did additional research. Validating Intel about Al-Qaida crossing the U.S./Mexico border was the primary objective of that Project, but discovering Arab speaking military types guarding drug-running operations through Mexico required further investigation.

It was already known that Hezbollah had established a military presence in Mexico close to the U.S. border, but there were no reports about them escorting drug shipments.

While using other sources to investigate the Hezbollah situation in Mexico, the Board had discovered a money trail from Iran that supported Hezbollah in Mexico and Hamas in Canada. The funds were first shipped to Grand Cayman for distribution and to help avoid detection, the house of a rich terrorist supporter was being used instead of an offshore bank.

Using seized money from previous Projects, information about the date of the next shipment was purchased and the Board had decided there was enough time to mount a Project to intercept the next shipment if the Team agreed. It would not cripple the terrorist operations, but it would slow them down for a while, especially when Iran would wonder where their money had gone. Of course, little tidbits of information would be supplied indirectly by the Boards' resources to suggest the money disappearing was an inside job.

JJ and Mac once again entered the Team meeting room, but this time, they had brought along two additional items. "We brought these rascals along so they wouldn't destroy the house while no one was at home," JJ said, as he and Mac put Sandy and Peeka onto the floor.

Since JC was still in the Com Shack, the meeting was delayed, so Peeka and Sandy went over to the group. After saying hello, it was playtime again and the two were wrestling and batting at each other. When it looked like Peeka was retreating, she turned, charged Sandy, and at the last second stopped, went up onto her hind legs, and playfully batted at Sandy who stood her ground.

"I've seen that move before, but that time, a bird almost had a heart attack," Bean commented, referring to Blue Jay's encounter with Peeka in the woods.

When Peeka came down from her two-legged stance, she turned around and took off with Sandy in hot pursuit. JC had entered the room as they were going out the doorway and quickly stepped aside warning, "Watch out, brawlers in the house!"

After watching the two for a few seconds, he exclaimed, "I've seen that move before, but that time, you almost gave a bird a heart attack. I've got it on video."

"Okay, are you two dick wads done? If you are, we have some serious business to conduct. Of course, when I say 'we,' I'm not including you two, as usual!" Blue Jay announced.

After everyone had a chuckle from remembering the video episode, the meeting was called to order.

JJ explained how the Board had followed up on the additional Intel the Teams had supplied and what their findings were. He continued with, "We felt that going into Mexico and attempting to eliminate the Hezbollah presence seemed to be a waste of time since they would be quickly replaced and that going after their financing may be a better avenue. We then discovered the Iran connection and the distribution point in Grand Cayman.

"That concludes my part, so if there are no questions, I'll turn it over to Mac for the operational portion," JJ concluded.

Since the presentation was clear and straightforward, there were no questions, so Mac took the podium.

"Morning people," Mac started and everyone responded. "As you all know, this Project is located in a part of the world that is familiar to us all. In fact, the distribution site is just a short distance down the coast from where all of the big cruise ships put in and the place where another Project led us to four years ago.

"We feel the Intel is reliable, but as you all know, it still has to be verified and up close if possible. The Board suggested in an effort not to expose any Team members and risk them being recognized from the earlier Project, others be used instead.

"Dunn suggested the MI-Six operative who was stationed on Grand Caymon four years ago and who Di unofficially asked to play a part in that Project.

"Another suggestion was the two operatives Di sent to play a small part in the Tortuga Project. They decided to get more involved and along with the MI-Six agent, who showed up uninvited, got themselves involved in a firefight with superior numbers.

"Bottom line, we recommend The Seal, Major Tex, and The Brit be used, especially since they performed so well together."

Mac then paused to get a reaction from the Teams and it was all positive.

"As a side note," Mac added, "Dunn said at the Board meeting that they are all excellent choices. We couldn't ask for better, plus, he would have the enjoyment of watching Di Flippi trying to get his people back to work. The last time these three were put together, it took Di weeks to get Major Tex and the Seal back into this country. He said the real fun was the excuses they came up with for not coming back while they were really just party hearty all over the Caribbean with the Brit."

"That alone qualifies them for the job," Panda said with everyone's approval.

Mac continued with the Board's general idea of how the operational part of the Project might proceed, and then called for questions.

After answering a few questions, Mac said, "Per SOP, if the Teams decide to accept the Project, JJ and I will return for the review of your plan."

"Now, we'll gather up the Brawlers and head for the house unless they have managed to knock down a wall in the Barn and are already waiting for us in the backyard."

———

After the meeting with JJ and Mac, the Teams decided to take on the Project and planning began. Since it was not the first operation for the Team in this part of Grand Cayman, getting up to speed didn't take long. Reflecting on their experiences during that Project, it was decided not to use the jet as their means of transportation for two reasons. Not enough time had passed since it was used, plus, the same faces would be on the plane after something had happened on the island. Using commercial transportation was suggested. Arriving separately at the airport, The Seal, Major Tex, and The Brit could supply them with the necessary gear and weapons, and then after they had completed their mission, they could depart on one of the many cruise ships that put in during the morning, then depart that evening. That was rejected for several reasons, but the cruise ships visiting would be put to good use.

After kicking around a few more ideas, it was decided that the Teams involvement would have to be totally clandestine and that included entry and exit of the area. The Teams had been working together on projects for over 10 years at locations around the world that included urban, mountain, desert, islands, and one even involved a seaplane during a project in Cuba, so they would have no problem with developing a plan that could be very complex or very simple.

———— · — ·· — ————

While the Teams were planning the operational side of the Project, Di Flippi and Dunn were meeting again and discussing his part. Since the Seal and Major Tex were already part of Di's section, there would not be a problem, but since the Brit was still part of MI-6, that could present a hitch. They first considered again sending Blue Jay and Bean to approach the Brit since they had a long history, but then Di suggested it might be better for the Seal and Major Tex to do it.

"Are you sure they wouldn't just take off and go party?" Dunn inquired with a smile.

"No, that only happens after a mission has been completed," Di assured him.

"I know," Dunn said, trying to hold back his laughter.

"You think it's funny don't you?" Di asked.

"No, not at all," Dunn replied, laughing.

"I guess you have forgotten how difficult it can be working at the Agency?" Di suggested.

"I beg to differ," Dunn replied. "I remember very well how difficult it can be. Another thing I can remember is how amusing you thought it was when I had problems with Blue Jay and Bean, so shit that goes around, comes around."

Since Di was now laughing, he had little success in convincing Dunn that he didn't find that amusing back then.

After the two had quieted down, Dunn said, "What a pain in the ass they are and one even works for a foreign intelligence service," then shook his head and laughed.

"They are good people, aren't they?" Di added.

"The best," Dunn agreed, then both smiled as they reflected on some of their past antics.

The two decided Major Tex and the Seal would contact the Brit and try to recruit him for a surveillance and Intel gathering assignment.

Hopefully, the Brit would agree, but if not, Major Tex and the Seal would proceed with what everyone thought was a dangerous assignment to gather Intel about terrorist funding being distributed from that house on Grand Cayman.

Having completed their meeting, the two decided to go for dinner at a restaurant in the town of Gettysburg and catch up on family and old friends. "So, when are you going to retire?" Dunn asked Di, as they walked.

"Good question," Di answered. "I could call it a day anytime, but every time I get up to it, I put it off again."

"How does Trudy feel about it?" Dunn inquired.

"After so many years of being married to me, she said, 'Just let me know when you're retired so I know what to tell people in case they ask.'"

"Sounds like she hasn't changed much." Dunn laughed.

"Not hardly," Di replied.

———————

Three dark figures cautiously approached the rear of a luxurious house along seven-mile beach on Grand Cayman, and then separated. One stayed in position while the other two took up positions to the left and right of the house, then all three just observed and made mental notes of the activities. The three were not close enough to the building to alert any security people or be picked up on a camera, but they were well within range of the night vision gear they were using to scan the area.

The Seal, Major Tex, and The Brit performed this same exercise for three nights prior to the day when cruise ships dropped anchor and thousands of tourists again invaded Grand Cayman for the day.

The following morning, the ships were again anchored offshore and boats were ferrying in the tourists.

Ron Wootters

About four hours after the ships had arrived, a rented compact pulled into the driveway of the luxurious house and an American got out. Asking for directions could have been one reason to stop, but stopping to admire the beautiful house was a better one, plus it gave the Seal a reason for looking around and to even look into the windows. It wasn't long before the Seal was joined by several big Arab looking men who were making inquiries about what he was doing.

The two men walking on the beach across the road from the house were in deep conversation and had stopped to continue their talk while one stood facing out to sea and the other faced in the direction of the house.

"I say, what is he up to now?" the Brit inquired.

"He's up there flapping around like a big Mary," Major Tex replied, describing how the Seal was pointing around at different things while the security people were telling him to leave.

"Hope he doesn't overstay his welcome," the Brit commented.

A short time later, two other men appeared from inside the house.

"One of the two men that just came out of the house could be the owner or the man in charge," the Major said. "Looks like they may be inviting him inside."

"Not good," the Brit said. "They may just illuminate him as a precaution, but let's see how it plays out before the British official and his security man go charging up there."

"How come I have to be the security man?" Major Tex inquired. "I can say 'quite so,' as well as you do."

"My dear Major, the way I say it and the way you say it is like comparing a painting by Rembrandt with a picture of dogs playing poker."

"Ho, that's funny. Yeah, Uppity Limey," Major Tex observed.

"Uppity Limey? Charming," the Brit replied. "You American chaps do have a way with words."

They were now getting rather insistent that he join them inside, but the Seal was declining and kept pointing down toward where the ships were anchored. He then produced a card and handed it to the man in charge who read it, moved away from the others, and took out a cell phone.

After a quick call, the man returned to the group and instructed the others to back away. After shaking hands with the man, the Seal got into his car, proceeded down the driveway, and then turned left in the direction of the cruise ships.

With the Seal now in the clear and after waiting a while, the two men on the beach also started walking back toward the cruise ships while Major Tex explained why he preferred dogs playing poker over that Rembrandt shit.

After making sure they were not being followed, the three men reassembled.

As the Seal approached the two men, Major Tex inquired, "So, where in the plan did it say you would flap around like a big Mary?"

"I say, a simple well done would have been nice, but this is much better," the Brit approved.

"Is that it?" the Seal inquired.

"Yeah, for now," the Major answered.

"How did you get free of those chaps?" the Brit inquired.

"I gave them a real estate agent card and told them I had a big Palooka on the hook and was trying to sell him something on Grand Cayman," the Seal replied. "That was my out if I got stuck and the number on the card was to a special phone on Di's desk. We did decide to keep you in mind when talking about the big Palooka to keep it real," the Seal informed Major Tex.

"Here's a suggestion," the Brit interrupted, "let's report in our findings."

"Good idea," Major Tex agreed. "Come on, flapping Mary, we have to go report in."

"Yes, sir, Major Palooka, sir," the Seal replied, as the three started walking.

"Things worked out jolly good actually. By the looks of those chaps, I don't think they would have been impressed with my fake credentials or my security man," the Brit observed.

"Still don't understand why I have to be the security man," the Major complained again.

"Have to go along with him on that," the Seal agreed. "It would be much more convincing to introduce him as, 'I say, this is my shit coolie.'"

The Brit was right about the security men at the house not being impressed, but other eyes were watching how things were unfolding and were ready to act if needed.

The Teams were getting daily updates, via Di, of all Intel gathered by the Seal, Major Tex, and the Brit including the flapping Mary incident. There was a lot more in the way of security measures than met the eye at a distance, plus evidence of more people onsite. That, plus with the people escorting the money, things could get interesting.

After they reported in, Di Flippi had thanked the Brit for his help and then instructed the Seal and Major Tex to return to Washington.

With their assignment completed and having been instructed several times by Di to return to Washington, Major Tex looked at the Brit and inquired, "So, where will we be partying this time?"

"Follow me," the Brit said, as he turned and started walking.

"I guess this means you'll be getting me into trouble again?" the Seal complained.

"Well, you can put all of the blame on me, flapping Mary," Major Tex replied.

"And I'm sure if I did, it would become at least a chapter in The Memoirs of Major Palooka," the Seal announced.

"Flapping Mary," the Major replied.

"Major Palooka," the Seal responded.

This bantering went on until the Brit came to a stop and the three were looking at a small fishing boat. "So, we're going fishing?" Major Tex inquired.

"Not exactly," the Brit answered.

"I get it, we're starting with a booze cruise," the Seal guessed.

"Not that either," the Brit replied, as he reached down, picked up a rope, and pulled the small boat closer to the beach.

With everyone aboard and the boat well underway, the Brit asked the Seal to take the wheel, went below, then reappeared with three AK-Sniper rifles.

"You want us to help you with something?" Major Tex inquired.

"No," the Brit informed him. "As you know, I'm an inquisitive sort of chap and there's something on this island that has me wondering."

"And the weapons?" the Seal inquired.

"Well, let's just say we'll get you chaps familiar with them and we'll have them along just in case. The AK-Sniper rifle is a jolly good weapon," the Brit assured the two and then said, "I have a marvelous story, using no names of course, about an experience I had with this weapon in Jamaica some years ago."

By the time the Brit had completed his story, they were far enough out to sea to let the two men get familiar with the weapons. The Brit tossed four empty one-gallon containers overboard, then turned the boat 180 degrees and after a while, came to a stop some distance away and said, "Realize the boat is bouncing a bit, but you should get the idea."

"So, this is the AK-Sniper rifle?" Major Tex said, as he picked up one of the weapons. "Where do the bullets come out?"

69

"Will you just load up?" the Seal suggested, as he inserted a magazine into one of the other sniper rifles.

"Now don't get me excited, flapping Mary, or I'll piss all over myself," the Major warned, as he picked up a loaded magazine.

The Brit and the Seal were already firing at the containers, as Major Tex placed the corner of the butt of his rifle into his shoulder, then rolled it tightly into place, held it tight with his right hand while relaxing the left. After taking three shots, he made corrections to the scope for elevation and windage, doped his scope, and was again taking aim. He fired a round hitting one of the containers, then fired another and hit a second. "Flapping Mary, you and the Uppity Limey can have the other two," Major Tex announced.

"Charming, just charming," the Brit replied, as he and the Seal became more intense about hitting their targets.

Chapter 7

Not knowing the exact number of security people in the house, plus how many would be escorting the money, it was decided that the long-range shooters and spotters would join the Team in the assault on the house.

After nightfall, the Team had assembled at a position about one half mile to the rear of the house and JC was again going over last minute details. Pru and Met would go with him to the right of the house and hold. Bean, Tic, Jockey and Bris would do the same to the left. Blue Jay, Benz, Panda and Check would approach from the rear of the house and try to establish if the money had already arrived.

When JC had finished, he asked, "Any questions?"

After a pause, Blue Jay said, "You know this looks a lot like Marine Corps fire team tactics."

"And your question is?" JC asked.

Before Blue Jay could say anything, Bean said, "I've heard about these tactics. Will we all get an opportunity to charge a machine nest holding a bayonet in our teeth?"

"Well, it's better than hanging out of a tree in the jungle and asking, 'Do you like my Green Tam,' as people pass by," Blue Jay answered.

"How do you know it's better, bayonet biter," Bean inquired.

"Okay, let's form a skirmish line," JC instructed.

The Team wished each other luck, then moved into position. Once the line was formed, JC said, "Com check," and then listened as the Team members replied in their usual sequence. That completed, JC said, "Move out," and the line moved forward.

They moved slowly and cautiously until they could barely see the house, then JC brought them to a halt. Using arm and hand singles, JC motioned the Team to break into three units and proceed.

From this point on, the three units moved even more quietly.

When JC and Bean were in position at the left and right, they sent a prearranged signal over the com. Once both signals were heard, Blue Jay, Benz, Panda, and Check moved in closer to the rear of the building. As they surveyed the area, outside lights came on.

"So much for snoopin' and poopin' in the dark," Blue Jay whispered into the com.

"Do you think you've been discovered?" JC inquired.

"If we were, people would have been coming our way by now," Blue Jay answered. "It's more like a security thing or they're expecting someone to arrive."

After a 10-minute wait, two cars pulled into the driveway; eight men came out of the house and assumed positions at each corner of the building.

Check had the long-range listening device in position and would focus on whoever seemed to be the most important person that had just arrived. Sometimes, a simple greeting could tell many things.

As the cars came to a stop, all of the doors on the first car opened, four men got out, walked back to the second car, and assumed security positions.

"No one of importance in the first car," Check said, as he aimed the device at the other car.

No one got out of the second car until two men appeared from inside the house, then one of the security men opened the left rear door and a man got out. As he walked toward the other two men, it was obvious he was not the money courier. As the two men greeted him, Check was listening very intently. "This is an important man, the money has arrived or both," he reported over the com.

When the two were done greeting him, the important man motioned toward the car for someone to join him and as another man started getting out of the car with a briefcase in hand, the front doors of the car swung open and two men appeared holding automatic weapons.

"Looks like the money has arrived," Check informed everyone and the wait began.

The eight men who had come out of the house stayed in position outside while the men who arrived with the money stayed with the money.

———————

While all of this was going on, the Seal and Major Tex were being guided to a vantage point where the Brit could satisfy that curiosity he had mentioned.

"Did we leave the island?" Major Tex inquired, complaining about the long walk.

"We have to take the long way round, chaps. Chin up and all of that," the Brit replied.

"I think you should change the Uppity Limey to the Nosy Limey," the Seal suggested.

"And put it into my memoirs, a long walk with a Nosy Limey," Major Tex added.

"Charming," the Brit replied. "It's not as charming as Uppity Limey, but still charming, especially that Limey part."

"Shouldn't complain though, it could be something much worse like Flapping Mary or Major Palooka. I say, did you come about that name by just putting Palooka after Major or are we looking at major as meaning something large?"

"What do you think?" the Seal inquired.

After looking at Major Tex, the Brit said, "Then Big Palooka it is."

"Watch it, that Nosy Limey change is just holding on by a thread," Major Tex informed the Brit.

The three chuckled at the exchange as they continued their journey to nosy lookout.

Due to time restraints, the Team couldn't wait until the early morning hours to start their assault, so after everything quieted down and they had given the new arrivals a chance to check out everything—and to also calm down after their long journey—JC was on the com. "Looks like the lights will not be going off, so we can get in closer. Taking out the security will be by my count."

All of the Teams' MP-5's were already silenced and each Team member was assigned a target.

With that completed, JC was again on the com. "Hit and move quickly. We can't afford an extended firefight. On three counting from one," JC instructed. Then JC counted slowly, one, two, three, and 11 silenced weapons fired and eight security men fell.

While those men were still in the process of falling, the Team members were up and moving toward their objective when they heard someone at the rear of the house sounding the alarm.

Ah shit, there's always some turd in the woodwork, JC thought, as they moved toward the house.

Soon after the alert was heard, men started coming out of the rear of the house and Blue Jay was on the com. "More than six just appeared and I don't think the six that arrived with the money are amongst them."

"Any activity on the left?" JC inquired.

"No, moving to reinforce the rear," Bean replied, as his unit moved quickly to assist their Teammates at the rear who were preparing to repel a head on assault.

To present less of a target for the 15 men, Blue Jay's unit had assumed prone positions and were waiting for the assault. They didn't have to wait long before orders were yelled out and Check said over the com, "They're starting their assault."

As the 15 started their attack, the unit held fire for a few seconds until the attackers were more in the open and away from possible cover. Blue Jay said, "Let's do it," and his unit along with Bean's unit, who had moved into position to the left of the attackers, opened fire, taking down at least half.

"Are you people in need?" JC inquired over the com.

"We're handling it," Blue Jay answered.

Knowing they didn't need additional help and that most of the people inside were focused on the activity at the rear of the house, JC moved his unit toward the right front corner of the house. Once there, they stayed low and prepared to make entry into the house when they saw three cars approaching at a high rate of speed. "Reinforcements may be arriving at the front," JC alerted everyone over the com.

The 23 men stationed at the house were backed up by an additional 15 positioned offsite.

While JC, Pru, and Met changed positions from assaulting the house to repelling new attackers, the other Team members went on the offensive.

The three cars approached at a high rate of speed, turned into the driveway, and stopped. Five men from each car piled out with weapons at the ready and moved toward the firefight at the rear of the house until JC, Pru, and Met brought them under fire.

"I say, that hardly seems fair, fifteen against three," the Brit informed the others, as they all watched the activities from nosy lookout.

"Maybe we should intervene?" the Seal suggested.

"That's why we have these weapons," the Brit answered. "It seems everyone in the world has an AK something or other and they are hard to trace."

"Maybe we should change your name to Clever Limey," Major Tex suggested.

"Charming," was the reply, as all three selected targets through their sniper scopes.

The unit was holding its own against the reinforcements, but JC noticed more of the opposition dropping than should be.

"Are any of your people assaulting the reinforcements?" he inquired over the com. "More seem to be going down than should be."

"No, but we'll be there shortly," Blue Jay informed him. "Don't worry, shit like that happens sometimes."

"Yeah, it happened to us once in Jamaica," Bean added.

Between the fire from nosy lookout and JC's unit, the firefight was being won at the front. Bean had also redirected Jockey and Bris to the firefight at the front and they were firing through the side windows to suppress any fire coming from the house.

With the reinforcements dealt with, JC turned again to the house entry and after coordinating with everyone, the assault began with flash bang grenades followed up with entry. Jockey and Bris had already downed two of the six guarding the money and the remaining four were quickly eliminated, but some of the people seemed to be unaccounted for. "Money man missing," JC alerted, as several muffled bursts from MP-5s were heard at the right side of the house.

"We have it," Benz reported over the com, as Panda cut the chain that secured the briefcase to the money man's wrist.

"Secure the area and turn off those outside lights," JC instructed. "Bring in that case so Check can inspect it for any booby-traps."

Everyone knew what to do; they secured the area and then searched for Intel.

Check found what looked like a serious bobby-trap and was very carefully disarming it on the dining room table. After it was disarmed, he discovered a secondary and said, "These people are serious about this shit. Hope there isn't just a nasty note inside." After the secondary was disarmed, Check continued opening the lid and searched for devices like pressure detonators that may be sitting on a thin slice of explosives at the bottom of the case. That completed, he notified the others that they could come in and as they did, he informed them, "There's over a million dollars here."

"The Board will be able to buy a lot of information with that," JC replied.

The case probably had a tracking device in it, so the money was put into four separate backpacks and then it was time to depart.

"Let's form up outside," JC instructed into the com.

Check and Bris were in position a short distance ahead of the others to try to avoid any surprises. After checking in both directions at the road and not seeing any oncoming headlights, they notified the others that it was safe to cross onto the beach. With JC leading, everyone walked in single file, as they moved across the beach toward the breakers. In order to cover up footprints in the sand, one man at the rear of the line pushed sand into the footprints followed by another with a small rake type device to smooth over the sand. To help distort the smoothing over of the sand, two others walked casually toward the beach leaving normal, someone out for a walk, footprints.

Halfway across the beach, JC said, "Has Dad arrived yet?" over the com.

"Dad is already here," a voice replied, as four rubber rafts appeared out of the darkness and headed toward the beach.

"Load up," JC ordered and the single file moved toward the rafts.

The waves splashed against JC's boots while he waited and then he watched as one by one, the Team members moved to the rafts. After one last look, he, too, moved to the rafts while saying, "Let's move out," over the com. As Top, LadyA, Lady1, and Mac gently revved the electric motors on the four rafts, a man at the front of each raft pushed to help get it off the beach. That completed, the men also jumped into the rafts and they were all underway.

Seeing the rafts were moving safely out to sea, the Brit commented, "Rather nice exercise, wouldn't you say?"

"I know they're on our side and have a feeling we have worked indirectly with them before, but who in the hell are they?" Major Tex inquired.

"Need to know and all of that," the Brit advised, then suggested, "Shall we go?"

"The long walk back," Major Tex grumbled.

"Maybe we'll take a shortcut on the way back," the Brit suggested.

"Good," the Seal remarked.

As the three departed the area, the Brit headed toward the sea. The other two stopped and inquired, "Isn't this the way?" as they pointed in the opposite direction.

"One never takes the same route on return," was the reply.

After a short walk, the three were standing on a ridge overlooking a beach that was deserted with the exception of a small boat.

"Gentleman, there is our transportation," the Brit announced.

"If it was this close, why did we take the long walk?" Major Tex inquired.

"Well, those chaps could have had long-range shooters about and if they thought we were the enemy, rounds could have been flying in our direction from every which way," the Brit explained.

"He's a Clever Limey," the Seal observed, as they all moved toward the beach.

"I say, can we reduce the two-word nicknames to one name? Like Flapping, Palooka, and I'll be Cleaver," the Brit suggested, then added, "Just joshing. In fact, I have a pleasant surprise for you chaps. I have arranged for a rather nice boat that sleeps six, is stocked with liquor, and has several beautiful party women we will rendezvous with a short distance out to sea."

"Really?" the Seal inquired enthusiastically.

"Heavens no. Where would I get the finances to do something like that?" the Brit inquired.

"He's a regular Limey of Jocularity, isn't he?" Major Tex announced.

"I'd say he's more like what goes into a jock," the Seal corrected.

"Good one," Major Tex approved, as he and the Seal bumped fists.

"Charming," the Brit commented, having a hardy laugh.

The Brit did have a rather nice boat waiting, so they could sail around the Caribbean in party hardy mode, but he was having too much fun to tell them about it just yet.

———

The four rafts rendezvoused with a yacht miles out to sea and then after weighting them down, the four rafts were sunk.

That completed, the Teams went below and started analyzing the Intel they had gathered.

"According to this document, one point five million was to be sent to Hezbollah in Mexico and point five million to Hamas in Canada. So, two million dollars was in that case," Check announced.

"If there's one thing the Board likes doing, it's buying terrorists' secrets using terrorists' money," JJ added.

Chapter 8

After the Grand Cayman Project, the Team finally got to go on leave and were returning to the Barn from their time off.

All of the Team members hadn't returned yet and since Blue Jay and Bean only saw their old mentors during the planning and execution of a Project, they thought this might be a good opportunity to spend some quality time with them. Jar Head and Doggie were there trainers during their Agency time and Swabbie was the boss of all four.

The duo thought a daytrip to the James A. Michener Museum in New Hope, Pennsylvania would be a good opportunity to catch up and were on their way to pick the three men up, but first, they stopped at the house for some mischief making.

As the duo walked across the lawn toward the kitchen door, Bean noticed Peeka and Sandy were very focused on a small hole in the ground.

"Wonder what they're up to now," Bean said aloud.

"They're watching a mole hole; if one comes up, they get it," Blue Jay explained.

"No shit," Bean exclaimed then yelled, "Watch out, moley, they're gunning for ya."

"You could learn something from them because you have the focus of a June bug," Blue Jay advised.

As usual, the two started exchanging one-liners, but then observed Top, JJ, and Mac through the window sitting at the counter and decided to continue their battle later.

"This couldn't have worked out better if we planned it," Blue Jay said to Bean.

Once inside, Bean inquired to Top, "Are the Ladies around?"

"Ladies, you have visitors!" Top yelled out and seconds later, Lady1 and LadyA appeared in the kitchen.

"Good morning, Ladies. Hope you rested well last night?" Blue Jay inquired.

Not knowing what the two were up to, but knowing it was probably not good, Lady1 answered, "Thank you, rested very well," with her voice suggesting there was a reason for them resting very well.

"We were just heading out for the day, but wanted to tell you we priced those kitchen cabinets and Anderson windows we saw at Niece's Lumber in Lambertville and think they're good deals," Bean told the Ladies.

"We know how fussy you both are about wood stain, so we inquired and there's a man onsite that is very good with stain finishes," Blue Jay added.

"That's good, maybe we can go take a second look to see if we still like them and maybe talk with the man about the different stains," LadyA replied.

"Okay, we have to go, we're running late. We'll talk later," Bean said, as he and Blue Jay turned to leave.

When the duo were back in the car, Bean said, "That should stir up things a little."

"I'd say by the look in the Ladies' eyes, they'll add to it."

While the duo made their observations, JJ inquired, "The house doesn't need new cabinets or windows, does it, Top?"

"Not that I can see," he replied.

"They're not for here," LadyA informed JJ.

"For who then? Jar Head, Doggie or Swabbie?" Mac asked, getting very inquisitive.

"No, no, and no," Lady1 replied, as the Ladies turned and left the kitchen.

The conversation now had Top wondering and he yelled out, "Well, who are they for then?"

"We'd rather not saaay," LadyA sung out from the hallway, as Lady1 put both hands over her mouth, so they wouldn't hear laughter back in the kitchen.

The three men just sat quietly for a while then JJ said,

"Mac, you're the one who said, 'That means Blue Jay, Bean, and the Ladies can double date.' Then later I said, 'They may be busting our balls, but what if it develops into something more? Stranger things have happened.' Now what do you have to say?"

"I think it's Top Kiner's fault," Mac defended, as Top reacted with surprise. "When he said, 'and don't you guys get handsie with the Ladies,' he probably gave them the idea to fool around. If he had kept his mouth shut, they would have just gone to dinner and then returned home."

"That's real thin," JJ replied while looking at Mac.

"Too thin?" Mac asked.

"Too thin," JJ confirmed. "Try again and please don't ask me again if I remember Sunny Sands."

"Sunny Sands! Ho, I wouldn't even think about bringing that name up again. You really lost it big time when I mentioned that name before," Mac assured JJ.

After saying that, Mac sat quietly until JJ said, "Well, nothing more to say?"

"Sorry, I was deep in thought," Mac answered. "I'm starting to get real concerned about your memory. I'll bet you don't even remember that freedom fighter on Tortuga? Just because it was a deserted island, it doesn't mean they can't have Freedom fighters."

"That's it, words fail me," JJ exploded. "Do you have any weapons handy?" he asked Top Kiner who handed him the big spoon he had used on Jockey.

"Ya traitor ya," General Mac reprimanded Top.

"False blame gets the big spoon," Top explained.

"Never trust a non-com," Mac said, as he quickly moved toward the kitchen door.

Bean, Blue Jay, and their mentors were driving down Bridge Street in Lambertville en route to the Mitchner Museum when they heard sirens approaching from behind them. Bean looked into the rearview mirror then said, "Guess I better pull over."

Once parked at the curb, the five watched as fire engines raced past responding to an alarm.

"These fire companies have some neat names," Blue Jay observed. "Union, Hibernia, Fleetwing, Columbia."

"And their equipment is very well maintained," Bean noticed.

"The men and women who make up those fire companies are all volunteers," Doggie informed him, "and those people," he added, pointing at the Lambertville/New Hope ambulance and rescue squad vehicle, "have won at national competitions in the past."

"Do these people cover up around where you all live?" Bean inquired.

"No, but we're in good hands," Jar Head answered. "The Stockton Fire Company covers our area, but if needed, these companies will assist them."

"When we were planning to have our homes built, we looked into the area firefighting capabilities," Swabbie informed Bean and Blue Jay. "Each town has a fire department whose primary responsibility is that town, but they also back each other up if called upon. Lambertville, Stockton, Mount Airy, and New Hope,

Pennsylvania across the river are within about four miles of each other. If additional help is needed, Sergeantsville, Ringoes, Flemington, Titusville, and others will respond."

"Does that also apply for rescue?" Blue Jay asked.

"I believe so," Doggie replied. "Lambertville also has a powerboat for river rescues so they're called upon from up and down the river."

"Not bad," Bean approved.

The fire trucks had turned off leaving the street clear and allowing the trip to proceed.

One block to the bridge, across the river to New Hope, Pennsylvania up the hill, and then Bean turned right into the driveway of Union Square. He then proceeded to the back where the museum was located. When they arrived, there was no sign of a Michener Museum.

"This is good," Jar Head started. "Invite us out for the day, and then screw up."

"The museum was here," Bean and Blue Jay insisted.

"Yeah, yeah, was here," Doggie added, as all five men got out of the car.

"We'll go ask someone," Blue Jay and Bean told the others.

Five minutes later, the duo returned and Bean announced, "Okay, here's the scoop. We asked inside New Hope Fitness and they said the museum had closed some time ago, but there's another Michener Museum in Doylestown, Pennsylvania. It's only about fourteen miles west of here, so we'll just continue on."

The three men listened and then moved toward the car. As they were about to get back in, the whistle blew on a steam locomotive at New Hope and Ivy Land Railroad not far from where they were standing.

When the whistle stopped, Jar Head announced, "Those old time steam locomotives are neat."

"So, now I guess your father wants to go for a ride on the choo-choo?" Bean asked Blue Jay.

With that, Jar Head looked at Doggie and asked, "When you were that dickhead instructor at the Agency, didn't you teach him to respect his elders?"

"Mine? What about yours?" Doggie said, pointing toward Blue Jay. "He's not exactly something you should get instructor of the year for."

"Yeah, you're right. They're both cut from the same cloth, no good."

"We do respect our elders," Blue Jay defended, "but we draw the line at ancients."

"So, now we're ancients?" Doggie asked Jar Head and Swabbie.

"Maybe we all can discuss this during the ride to Doylestown," Swabbie suggested, knowing if he didn't get everyone into the car and underway, the four would probably be in a verbal battle until nightfall.

They were about a mile into their trip when Bean put on his right turn single. "Are we in Doylestown already?" Doggie inquired.

"Top Kiner asked me to pick up something at the Delray True Value store," Bean answered.

Bean had parked the car and was about to get out when Jar Head said to Doggie, "Hope they don't screw this up like they did the Michener thing."

"Yeah, what are the odds of something like that happening twice in a row?" he replied.

"I'll come with you," Blue Jay said to Bean. "After we get the stuff for Top, we'll stop by the CVS and get some strong pain killers for the big pain in the ass I seem to be developing."

"Or we could buy two hammers at Del Ray and treat the cause," Bean suggested.

As Bean and Blue Jay walked away from the car, Jar Head said, "These kids are getting better at this shit aren't they?"

"Looks that way," Doggie agreed with a smile. "What can we get on their asses about when they come back?"

"Knew I should have declined the offer to come along," Swabbie said, shaking his head. "Maybe you should give them a break?"

With that, Jar Head looked at Doggie and inquired, "Maybe he's right. Maybe we should layoff. Instead, we'll tell them about the time we stayed at the Lambertville House back in the nineties and all of the shit that other guy did."

"Yeah, that may be of interest to them, dropping water filled condoms onto a motorcycle club, the police coming. Boy, was he wasted," Doggie added.

Swabbie listened then asked, "So, what can we get on their asses about when they come back?"

"We were wondering if you recognized the Lambertville House when we drove past it," Doggie said and all three burst into laughter.

——— —— ——

Planning, preparation, and execution of two smaller Projects were conducted during the months that followed Grand Cayman. It was now late November and the Team members were due back at the Barn within the week.

Gil Dunn was in his office busy running the company when his private phone rang. Not liking to be disturbed when he was very busy, Dunn reluctantly answered it with a simple, "Yes."

"Hello, how are things going?" a familiar voice inquired.

"Okay, how about yourself?" Dunn answered, already knowing it probably wasn't good.

"I'm all right now, but think I got a touch of food poisoning from a piece of peach pie I had at dinner the other night."

"Sorry to hear about that," Dunn said, knowing what Di was really referring to. "Should we reschedule our get together?" Dunn inquired.

"No, I feel pretty good now, but wanted to let you know in case I have to cancel," then after some small talk, Di said, "So, I'll be seeing you on Wednesday night, around eight P.M., okay?"

"Sounds good," Dunn agreed, then ended the conversation.

I knew it, Dunn thought. *Peach pie means meeting location will be in the peach orchard at*

Gettysburg. Now for those bullshit CIA gyrations to figure out the real date and time of the meeting.

Since Di Flippi and Dunn were using the same bullshit CIA gyrations that Dunn had established when he was the DDO at the CIA, Gil had little problem in figuring out the real meeting was the following morning at 10:00 A.M.

———————

It was a mild fall morning at the peach orchard. Dunn walked to join Di Flippi who seemed to be in deep thought as he looked toward the peach orchard.

This time of year, the Gettysburg Battlefield Park doesn't draw the number of people as the summer months, but there are still tourists, some visitors within driving distance, and all are trying to comprehend what happened those three days in July 148 years ago.

As Dunn approached Di, he inquired, "Thinking about what happened here during the battle or the shit I know you're going to put in my lap."

"As I remember, it was your shit first," Di quickly answered, as he turned toward Dunn.

"You got me there," Dunn said with a smile, then questioned, "We gave the Feds a nice little package containing what looked like a terrorist plot, so what's the problem? Did they send the package back because you CIA ass wipes didn't put a nice little bow on the package?"

"Well, first, here's one of those illegal cigars you always reprimand me about before you smoke it. And second, don't forget you used to be a CIA ass wipe, and since you were the Deputy Director of Operations, I guess that made you the main ass wipe," Di continued.

Dunn replied, "Give in, give in."

After a long puff on the Cuban cigar, Di said, "It wasn't the FBI, it was some politically appointed asshole at justice who pulled the plug. They claimed since no real intelligence was being developed and due to budget considerations, the resources being used could no longer be justified."

There was a moment of silence, then a big puff of cigar smoke rose into the air over Dunn's head as he said, "Sometimes, I have to wonder whose side some of those people are really on."

"Have to agree. Claiming it's because they're liberal can only go so far, and then it becomes super stupid naiveté or just being a traitor to your country," Di said, followed by another big puff of cigar smoke rising into the air over his head.

"Did the non-political types share anything with you?" Dunn inquired.

"Since I gave them the lead in the first place, they were very accommodating with supplying up to date information. As we already know, people are crossing the border and being picked up in the desert by dune buggies. The FBI files stated they are then transported to Route Eight where they're picked up by a vehicle that changes in make and model with each pick up.

"Now here's where it gets interesting." Di became very serious. "The courier is taken to the train station where he boards an east bound train to Chicago, then the individual boards a train to Pittsburg. After arriving at Union Station in Pittsburg, they were picked up and taken to a farm outside of, ready for this, Lancaster, Pennsylvania. That's about fifty miles from this spot."

"Well, the courier should be easy to spot. Arab looking guy driving a horse drawn Amish carriage," Dunn remarked with a smile.

"Anyway!" Di continued, ignoring Dunn's humor. "The FBI kept the Farm under close surveillance and the report stated after a few days, the couriers start their journey back to Mexico.

"Pictures and video were taken of people who visited the Farm and through a process of elimination; people of interest were narrowed down to four visitors. Three of the four turned out to be local merchants just doing business with the Farm. The fourth raised suspicions, but then the plug was pulled on the case due to financial review by Washington."

"Sounds like those political types at justice took Harry Truman's saying, 'The buck stops here,' literally," Dunn observed, then was quiet for a few seconds.

"How can they call it quits due to costs on a case that started on the Mexico/California border, traveled across the country, and stopped in Pennsylvania?"

"Apparently, they had a cost results review and if the cost was high and the results were low, the case was dropped," Di replied.

"Even though the case may have developed to a point where a ton of results may have been very close," Dunn commented.

"Even though," Di confirmed.

"I'm almost afraid to ask this question," Dunn again spoke. "Did they or are they planning to hit the tunnel?"

"No, that's some of the good news. They're just maintaining half-ass passive surveillance," Di said.

"Do we have any information on that person who raised suspicion at the Farm?" Dunn asked.

"Yes, we do," Di replied. "The individual traced back to a cargo ship company."

"Cargo ship company?" Dunn remarked. "I can see why the FBI was interested."

"I'm sure you'll figure it all out," Di said, as he handed Dunn another cigar and said, "For later."

As Dunn looked at the cigar, he could see Di was using it to conceal a computer flash drive he was passing to him. "Thanks, I'm sure I'll enjoy it," Dunn said, as he grasped both the cigar and flash drive with his right hand and then put them into the inside pocket of his jacket.

"The way things are shaping up, I have a feeling this is going to be something big," Di Flippi offered.

"Feel the same," Dunn agreed.

"If you need people, the Seal and Major Tex from my staff are available. I'm sure the Brit could also be recruited again if needed, unless you're against it."

"No, the Brit is a good choice," Dunn agreed. "Came to know about him when I was still DDO at the Agency.

Dunn could see Di was a little puzzled so he said, "Remember when Blue Jay and Bean went out for revenge when they thought Jar Head and Doggie were set up and killed?"

"Ho, yeah, I remember that!" Di confirmed.

"Things were moving so fast back then maybe I didn't fill you in on all of the facts?" Dunn confessed.

"First let me say the few times I've thought about this, about halfway through, I wanted to kill myself. So, if I take out my gun and point it to my head, don't stop me."

"That bad?" Di said with a laugh. "I know they pulled some stuff."

"Pulled some stuff! You have no idea," Dunn exclaimed. "Every morning when I wake up, I'm still surprised I'm not in prison. Let me take that back, I'm still surprised Blue Jay and Bean are not in prison, and since they worked for me, am surprised I'm not under the prison." Dunn continued his story with reactions from Di varying from laughter, to shocked surprise, followed by more laughter.

———————

When Dunn had received the peach orchard call from Di Flippi, he figured the Project was coming back their way, so he asked JJ to call a Board meeting for the morning after he returned from Gettysburg.

The Board had been in session for about 30 minutes while Dunn informed the Board about all that was covered in his meeting with Di Flippi.

When Dunn had finished, JJ opened the meeting for questions and discussion.

"So, let me see if I have all of this straight," Wilson started. "The Team verified Dawson's Intel was correct. We indirectly turned it over to the Feds who tracked the couriers from California to a farm in Pennsylvania and were in the process of checking out a person of interest when the political appointees in Washington pulled the plug?"

"That's about it," Dunn agreed.

"So, will we be reactivating the recon Project or start from scratch with a new one?" Wilson then inquired.

"I guess we can answer that question right now with a show of hands," JJ said. "All in favor of reactivation?" When everyone raised their hands, "Reactivation it is," he confirmed. "Now how do we proceed?"

"Since the couriers traveled over two thousand miles across the country to Pennsylvania, it looks like they are targeting the east coast," John Howard observed.

"That's a good possibility," Dunn agreed, "but I'd say anywhere between Boston and Washington, D.C. would be a good guess, but anywhere on the east coast must be considered."

"I guess we should kick off a planning session," JJ suggested. "This Project started with Intel about possible border crossings and seems to be growing into something much, much bigger. I'm sure the other members join me in expressing our thanks to you, Dawson, for bringing this to our attention." Then JJ paused, as the other Board members acknowledged Dawson.

"Would you care to kick off the session?" JJ asked Dawson.

"I didn't know for sure, but had a feeling this Project would come back to us, so I started planning when the Team verified the Intel was correct," Dawson informed the others, as he produced a folder.

"Funny thing you're saying that," Wilson said, producing a folder, as did the other Board members.

"Seems like we were all on the same page without even talking about it," Dawson observed then continued.

"I would like to suggest we bring in Jar Head, Doggie, and Swabbie for additional analysis support. I realize we've done this more than once in the past and more than once, they seem to have gotten involved with the operational part as well."

"Can't hold that against them since the Board also seems to sometimes get involved with the operational part," JJ added.

The Board members smiled, as they reflected back to their last active involvement during a Project when everyone was active in the operational part.

"Firefights followed by a day at the boat races, what a Project," Howard said with a smile.

"You can say that again," Wilson added and everyone burst into laughter.

Since the Board members were all up to speed concerning the Project, JJ said, "Looks like our first objective is to find out more about High Seas Shipping Co., Ltd."

"I know if the FBI had those people under surveillance, they have a lot of pictures. Did Di supply you with pictures of the shipping company person?" Admiral Fox, or Foxie as everyone liked to call him, inquired.

"We do have pictures and a lot more," Dunn replied, as he removed the flash drive from his pocket that Di Flippi had passed to him.

"Excellent," Foxie approved.

"I guess we'll pick up where the FBI left off with the cargo ship company?" Mac said. "If that doesn't pan out, it's back to the Farm outside of Lancaster."

"That's true," Dunn affirmed, "but before we take any action in this country, I'd like to have the cargo ship company headquarters in Malta checked out. Since I have access to resources, I'll handle that part of the Project myself and report the findings."

JJ took a quick vote and all agreed for Dunn to conduct the investigation.

It wasn't the first time that Dunn had intelligence gathering and other things done with or without the Board's knowledge. When the Board and Teams started taking on projects, Dunn would on occasion use his old friend from when we he first became a CIA field operative. Rene was in French Intelligence, also new to fieldwork, and after first butting heads, Dunn and Rene decided to work together since they were both on the same side and developed a strong friendship.

During one of the tasks Dunn had given Rene, he was having a lot of trouble getting access to the information, but finally succeeded after contacting a retired KGB officer. The two developed a quick friendship, so Rene recruited him for future tasks. If one listened to their conversations, they might wonder about the relationship part, but that was just normal conversation between the two.

Dunn almost had a coronary when Rene told him he had recruited Boris. Not due to him recruiting someone, but because Boris was Dunn and Rene's archrival in the KGB during the Cold War years. After the initial shock and since the results were so good, Dunn became more at ease with the arrangement and from that point on, Dunn had an excellent team he could call on to perform tasks.

Chapter 9

Rene and Boris both enjoyed their retirements in Switzerland and with the exception of the occasional task from Dunn, they usually just did retirement stuff and that's what Boris was doing as Rene approached, sitting quietly looking at the distant mountain peaks.

"The answer is no," Boris said to Rene.

"How do you know if I have a question?" Rene inquired. "We talk every day and I don't always have questions."

"I can tell by the look," Boris replied. "I call it 'The Frog Tell' look."

"Well, you're wrong, Cossack," Rene quickly answered. "I just came over to say hello and chat. You know, the way we do every day? I come over here or you come to my house. You do remember that's what we do, don't you? I know you're getting soft in the head, so I just want to make sure."

Boris had a big smile on his face and just kept looking at Rene until he stopped talking, then asked, "So what and where is the task this time?"

"How do you do that?" Rene asked.

"It's, 'The Frog Tell,'" Boris again explained.

"Really?" Rene asked. "So what's the Frog telling you now?" he inquired, giving Boris the finger.

After a hearty laugh, the two got serious, as Rene relayed the what and where for the task.

Dunn wanted Rene and Boris to check out the Ship Company's main office in Vittoriosa, Malta. Since going in during working hours might get them on video tape from surveillance cameras, Rene and Boris decided to make a visit around 3:00 A.M. so they could conceal their identity, plus they would be able to get a closer look at the company's operations.

Four days after they had completed their planning and were navigating through back alleys on their way to the main office of High Seas Shipping Co., Ltd. The duo had walked past the building the day before checking it for cameras and other security. Not seeing any cameras, they thought the building had high-tech equipment or nothing.

The two observed the building for a brief time, then put on masks to hide their faces. "Who said Cossacks don't have a sense of humor?" Rene said, looking at Boris who was wearing a Nixon Halloween mask.

"Two Nixons breaking into an office," Boris replied. "I wonder if they know who Nixon was? Wouldn't want all of this humor to go to waste."

Rene shook his head and smiled at the comment. One thing for sure was that Boris didn't lack a sense of humor. In fact, it was his idea about wearing the Nixon masks.

After drawing their silenced weapons, Rene slowly moved to the building while Boris watched for any movement at the windows of the building. After arriving at a window, Rene quickly checked for any security around the windows, then motioned for his partner to join him. When Boris arrived at the window, Rene informed him, "I can't see any security. See what you think."

Boris inspected the window thoroughly. "I can't see anything around the window. Let me check something else," he said, removing a pair of glasses from his pocket and putting them on. After scanning the room through the window, Boris reported, "I don't see any beams that upper class security systems use."

"Something is screwed up about all this," Rene observed.

"I agree," Boris said, then added, "Shall we?" as he motioned toward the window.

After Rene shook his head in agreement, Boris quickly unlocked the window and started to raise it up when Rene said, "I hope the building doesn't blow up. Suicide vests, suicide bombers…maybe this is a suicide window?"

"Tricky Dick, you are too funny," Boris replied, as he continued to raise the window.

Boris took a quick look inside the window, then after Rene took one last look around the outside area, the two men entered the building.

Once inside, the two put on night vision gear, then started to inspect the building. Assuming the room they were in wasn't being used, they moved through the remainder of the first floor, then performed the same procedure on the second floor. Once that was completed, Rene motioned they leave the building. Boris shook his head in agreement and the duo departed.

The two kept their masks on and took even more precautions than when they had arrived.

When they were a good distance away, Boris said, "Two things are very obvious. One, since the building was empty except for the front entrance area, it's a front for a non-existing company and they're crooks or something else. Two, they may be watching the building in case someone comes looking."

"Well, if the latter is the case, they've probably called for help," Rene added.

Taking a different route when departing was SOP, but the two added more turns, stops and starts in case someone was trying to follow. Problem was, if anyone was trying to follow, they probably knew the area very well, where Rene and Boris didn't.

Boris was in the lead and had made a quick turn into a narrow street with Rene close behind when a round whizzed past Rene's head and slammed into a wall across the street. The duo immediately went into a kneeling position as they checked out the area. "Well, I didn't hear any gunfire, so I guess we can assume they're not street hoods," Rene observed.

"They probably think we'll run down this alley, but we won't," Boris stated.

"We won't?" Rene questioned.

"They probably have some of their friends waiting for us down there and will try to catch us between them, so we'll have it out with those who are pursuing us."

"We will?" Rene questioned again. "What if there are a lot of them with automatic weapons?"

"Don't worry about that," Boris assured Rene.

"Really? Well, you might want to stand up first if you're going to pull a machine gun out of your ass," Rene suggested.

"No machine gun, something much better," Boris replied, as he produced a round object from his inside pocket. "I had this developed when at the KGB, it's very effective."

Just then, the two men could hear footsteps moving quickly down the street and Boris said, "Get ready."

Staying in his crouched position, Rene got very close to the corner of the building while Boris stood and prepared to throw the weapon that would even the odds.

When the footsteps sounded very close, Boris quickly looked around the corner of the building and then threw the round object at the five men. At first, nothing happened, then the round object started to fizzle, then bright flashes followed by colored sparks flying in all directions. "Now!" Boris alerted Rene and both men opened fire, downing two men with their first two shots, shortly followed by another two. The fifth man threw away his piston, then produced an automatic weapon from under his coat and started firing. Boris and Rene jumped back behind the building as rounds sprayed the area.

"This man is no professional," Boris observed. "Instead of short bursts, he's using up all of his ammunition."

"No shit," Rene replied, then continued with, "That wasn't a weapon, was it?"

"No," Boris answered.

"It was a toy, wasn't it?" Rene inquired.

"Yes," Boris confirmed, as the gunfire suddenly stopped and he and Rene quickly looked around the corner, then both fired their weapons, taking down the shooter in the middle of a reload.

"We must go," Boris said and started to move.

"Is that what we have to do?" Rene questioned. "Well, speaking for myself, I'd like to talk about the toy thing."

"We're still alive aren't we? And I didn't have to pull a machine gun out of my ass," Boris answered.

"No, you didn't," Rene agreed. "Instead, you used a secret weapon that you probably pulled out of a clown's ass at the circus."

After many more turns, stops, and starts it seemed, in spite of Rene's bitching about the secret weapon, the two were in the clear, so they proceeded to a pier where they had an alternate mode of transportation. While Rene boarded and started the motor on the small boat, Boris quickly untied the lines and within seconds, the boat was underway.

"A fucking toy. Maybe that Tricky Dick mask had a bad affect on you or maybe I should just call you Tricky Prick," Rene continued complaining.

"You're still alive, so just say thank you," Boris said with a smile.

"Just say thank you!" Rene repeated calmly and then added "Thank you, Tricky Prick!"

———————

Two days after their encounter in Malta, Rene and Boris were talking with Dunn in Brussels, Belgium. After their initial report, Gil had decided he wanted a more detailed report and that would have been too risky to conduct by phone, even a secure line, so he arranged to meet with them in person.

After Boris and Rene gave him a very detailed report, Dunn asked, "So, what are your assessments about High Seas Shipping Company?"

Rene started. "As we all know, it's just a front for something, question is for what?"

"I feel it's more than a front for a criminal enterprise," Boris added. "For one thing, why keep the building under watch twenty-four seven to protect nothing?"

"If it's a criminal activity, they would have tried to capture us and try to find out why we broke in instead of trying to kill us without warning."

We feel this is an Intel or terrorist operation," Rene continued. "As for what flavor of Intel or terrorist organization, there was nothing in the building to give us a clue. As for the weapons they used, they could have been purchased anywhere."

"As usual, you both have done an excellent job and have supplied a piece that fits right into a current puzzle," Dunn approved.

Since the beginning, Dunn, Rene, and Boris worked on a strictly need to know basis and all liked it that way. Dunn supplied the retired Intelligence Agents with information to perform a task; they were paid very well to execute very dangerous tasks, but were never told about the big picture or why Dunn wanted the tasks performed.

"If we're finished here, why don't I take you two out for dinner?" Dunn offered.

"Excuse me if we have already covered this," Rene replied, "but did I tell you about that secret weapon that Boris pulled out of a clown's ass at the circus?"

"If I knew you were going to go on and on about this, I would have let them kill you," Boris remarked.

"How can you say something like that?" Rene asked. "Tricky Prick!"

As the two continued their verbal battle, Dunn laughed and thought, *This is like home away from home.*

Chapter 10

Two days after Dunn's meeting with Rene and Boris, the Board was again in session concerning the current Project. Dunn had already told the other Board members about the empty building, but didn't go into too much detail about anything else except to say his sources were pursued and came under fire.

"Since the main office of the shipping company was empty, I'm sure the office outside of Philadelphia is the same. Getting Intel about a ship, if one does exist, will have to be done another way. The shipping company is just a front, but if someone wants it to look like a legitimate business, there must be a paper trail that can be looked into."

"We all know something big is going on, but I personally feel the size and scope may be a lot bigger than it appears."

When Dunn had finished, JJ said, "Gil, as usual, you have done an excellent job, especially when recommending we first check out the main office of High Seas Shipping Company prior to pursuing anything else on U.S. soil. If the Team went into that office in Pennsylvania, one of four things may have happened. It would have been a waste of time, a shootout would have occurred, if the FBI started up surveillance again our people would have been caught on video, and my personal favorite the Team on video tape during a firefight. Thank you, Gil, for possibly saving our collective asses." And the Board joined JJ in thanking Gil.

Dunn waved off any praise, saying, "Remember, that's what I used to do for a living."

JJ said, "We're now ninety-nine percent sure this is a terrorist operation and since it is on U.S. soil where we have to be concerned about being detected by law enforcement and the terrorists, how should we proceed?"

Foxie, the other former Intel type on the Board, offered his opinion. "Maybe a quiet visit to the Farm is in order? That was the destination for all of the couriers." The others agreed.

"So, we'll develop a plan and then present it to the Team?" JJ suggested.

"This is just a suggestion," Mac offered, "but since the Teams usually take our plans apart, then reassemble them after shit canning most of our ideas, I'd say we ask the Team how they want to go about it."

"I have to agree," JJ added. "I get the feeling they listen to Mac and my presentations out of pure politeness."

"The Teams and politeness," Mac laughed. "Do those two words go together?"

"Almost as bad as Teams and respectfulness, isn't it?" JJ added.

Everyone on the Board burst into laughter. They all knew and liked all of the Team members very much, but the truth was the truth.

————— —— ——

The following morning, JJ had given the Team all of the up to date information and it was Mac's turn to present the operational side of the Project. Mac was getting up to make his presentation, when JJ advised, "Be tactful."

"No problem," Mac confirmed.

"Morning all," Mac started. "The Board has decided since you change all of the plans we submit anyway, we'll just let you smart asses figure this one out from the get-go."

"And they wonder why the kids are all bad," JJ said aloud.

"Are there any questions, except from Jockey?" Mac continued.

Jockey immediately started whispering to Panda who was sitting next to him. When he was done, Panda raised his hand.

"Yes, Panda?" Mac acknowledged.

"Jockey wants me to ask why it took so long for you dick wads to come to that logical conclusion."

"Did I just hear the shot that will start another verbal battle?" JJ asked JC.

"My guess is, yes!" JC replied.

JJ then looked around the room until he saw Top Kiner and said, "Where can I buy one of those big spoons?"

Mac was in rear form as he and the Team went at it for about five minutes. When it finally calmed down, Mac got serious and called the meeting back to order. "So, how shall we proceed?" he again asked.

With that, JC stood and said, "We've already ran contingency plans about the Farm and the what-ifs that go along with it. What if the FBI has resumed surveillance? What if it's a terrorists' nerve center and they have a lot of security in and around the Farm? If this was a Project to take out the Farm, it would be one thing, but to get in and out again without being detected is something else."

The meeting went on for two hours and that was just the beginning of the planning for this part of the Project. When he thought it was probably time to call it a day, JC asked, "Are there any questions?"

Mac raised his hand and inquired, "So, you already have contingency plans?"

"Yes, we usually do that as an SOP," JC told Mac.

"I'll bet they have crib notes, too," Mac told JJ in a loud voice, "and that explains all of the quick comebacks to my humor."

"Big spoon, please!" JJ requested loudly.

The following day, JJ, Mac, and the Teams were in session all day and into the night planning the best way to get into and out of the Farm without being discovered by the bad guys inside or any good guys that may be watching from the outside.

Since this part of the Project would be conducted on U.S. soil, extensive measures would be taken and broken into three phases. For phase one, Jockey, JC, and Mac performed air reconnaissance using a small single engine aircraft. While Jockey flew the plane as slowly as possible in a south to north direction, JC and Mac were photographing the areas to the east and west. Once completed, the plane disappeared for approximately one hour and then returned flying east to west with pictures being taken to the north and south.

Flying in one direction while photographing areas on both sides of the aircraft was the same procedure the SR-71 spy plane used when it was in service, but it flew a little faster.

During one of the wars in the Middle East, both sides were making opposing claims that was holding up peace talks. The SR-71 took off from the U.S., flew to the Middle East, photographed the area in question, then flew back and landed in the U.S. Within a day, photographs were shown to the opposing forces resolving the claims and the peace talks continued.

The Teams were in the meeting room at the Barn going over photos taken from the poor man's SR-71 and had isolated areas that could be used for security monitoring purposes. It was very difficult to detect anything beyond the tree line, but the next phase would address that problem.

The following night, phase two was executed. Uncle Donald and the Tree Ducks along with the other members of the Team formed a skirmish line about one and a half miles from the Farm. All were equipped with com gear, night vision goggles, and after a com check, all started moving slowly into the tree line.

Once they reached the fields that surrounded the Farm and since nothing was detected, the Team changed course for the second objective, checking the tree line perimeter around the Farm. The 11-men skirmish line covered a wide enough area that would detect any surveillance or security. Any deeper into the heavily wooded forest would have made any security activity too difficult.

After making a 360-degree sweep of the Farm, JC brought the Team to a halt and said, "Looks like the Federal people were serious about pulling the plug on surveillance." The Team stayed in place and watched the Farm for any movement or security people until JC's voice came onto the com. "Let's form up."

With JC in the lead and taking a different route, the Team departed the area in staggered single file formation.

The following afternoon, Mac, JJ, and both Teams were again assembled in the meeting room and planning phase three.

"Phase one and two had gone well," JJ started the meeting. "We can be reasonably sure the FBI no longer has the Farm under surveillance and we haven't detected anything out of the ordinary with the Farm and that means they're keeping a very low profile or they're using very sophisticated security devices. So, now, we proceed with phase three?" JJ finished, motioning toward JC.

"The next time, we'll take a different approach and we'll be armed," JC started. "Phase two was primarily to detect any FBI presence, so we all were unarmed and took on the appearance of an amateur military type training exercise in case we were detected by any FBI in the area. For phase three, our long-range shooters/spotters will be on station, plus the remainder of the Team will be in support.

"Besides establishing there was no FBI presence during phase two, we noticed activity around one of the buildings that sits away from the others.

"We first wondered if it had something to do with the running of the Farm, but a person or persons would come out of the house, go into the building, and then later would reappear. This continued during the nighttime hours and for that reason, the building will be our primary focus.

"Question still to be answered is the time. The earlier we go in, the more danger of being discovered. If we go in later, there is less danger, but we also may get less Intel.

"The Teams have been discussing the pros and cons with some siding with going in later and photographing all documents then leave. Others like Mr. Stealth," the sounds of raspberries and other unfavorable sounds were heard coming from the Team, so Blue Jay stood and thanked everyone for their kindness, "thought it best we go in earlier," JC continued, "and attempt to pick up conversations, and then when everything quiets down, go inside and photo all documents."

"What if you don't speak their language?" Mac inquired.

"JC has a neat recording gizmo that can pick up conversations, even through glass," Blue Jay explained.

"How do you know about that?" JC inquired, as he looked at Blue Jay. "I haven't had it that long and didn't tell anyone about it."

"I was just practicing for the upcoming event," Blue Jay replied.

"I guess it would help to change the locks on the Com Shack," JC complained.

"Maybe if you got a young pit-bull and every morning showed it Blue Jay's picture, then smacked its ass with a rolled up newspaper, in a few months, the Shack would be secure," Mac offered.

"What would you do then?" Bean inquired to Blue Jay.

"I would just wear a General Mac mask," Blue Jay replied, "but then the dog would probably try to hump my leg."

"Well, I don't want to mention any names, but someone is of the opinion that you're a sissy boy," Mac replied.

"Don't even try to start. Peeka already told me she didn't say that and you were just putting words in her mouth," Blue Jay replied.

Mac looked at JJ and Top and said, "Okay, it had to be one of you."

"Not necessarily," JJ replied. "I saw that freedom fighter Sunny Sands around here the other day looking for ammo for those guns you gave him, so maybe he told Blue Jay?"

———

It was decided an early entry would be attempted and two nights later, the Team was in position just outside the tree line, as Blue Jay very slowly made his way across the open field behind the building that had all of the activity during their prior visit. Moving across the field like a sniper stalking his prey, Blue Jay moved very low to the ground or crawled until he was very close to the building, then waited and scanned the building for cameras or other security devices.

JC and the snipers/spotters watched Blue Jay's immediate area while the other Team members watched the house and the remainder of the area for any movement.

When Blue Jay didn't detect any security devices, he moved up next to the building and listened. When no voices were detected, he moved close to the right rear corner of the building, got into a prone position, and crawled the remaining few feet to the corner, then slowly looked around the corner checking for security devices. When none were seen, he continued a slow crawl toward the next corner of the building at the same time listening for voices. If Blue Jay continued around the next corner, he would pass the entrance, which was not a good place to be if someone suddenly came out of the building, so he backtracked until he was at the left rear corner of the building and continued. *Maybe no one is in the building yet,* Blue Jay thought. *It looks dark inside, but they could have something over the windows?* His thoughts were interrupted by the muffled sounds of voices coming from the building. After listening for a few seconds, he knew more than two people were in the building and continued moving, trying to find a place where he could hear the voices more clearly, but instead, the voices seemed to fade. Realizing that he backtracked to a point where the voices were the strongest, he searched the side of the building then ground alongside the building, but saw nothing out of the ordinary. In fact, the only thing that wasn't part of the building itself was an electric power meter. Blue Jay went to the meter, checked it out more thoroughly, and discovered a vent behind it. *Well, that explains why everything is dark inside. They're underneath the building.*

He put his ear close to the vent, but the voices were still too muffled to hear what they were saying. Blue Jay paused for a second, then whispered on the com. "They're under the building and I can't make out what they're saying. The listening gizmo is too large, but my com unit will fit into the vent. I'll lower it into the vent, but you'll have to listen and record at your end."

"Roger," JC replied. He went into one of his pockets and produced a very small recorder.

"You'll be off the com, so be on extra alert," he advised, as he repositioned the long-range shooters and spotters. Met and Panda were already covering Blue Jay, and Pru and Benz moved to a better vantage point so they could also cover that side of the building and their Teammate.

Blue Jay removed his com unit and very carefully inserted it into the vent, then lowered it as far as possible. He had no way of knowing if the voices could be heard on the com, but had to maintain his position in case they were.

The voices over the com were speaking in Arabic and JC was recording every word.

About an hour had passed when Blue Jay thought he heard the sound of a door opening. A few seconds later, a man appeared at the left front corner of the building. *If this guy is going to patrol the area, I'm in a bad position,* he thought to himself.

"Someone's going outside for a smoke," Check informed everyone on the com.

"We got him," both long-range shooters reported.

"Looks like he's bitching about something," Benz reported.

"He does look pissed," Panda agreed.

Check had already aimed the long-range listening device at the man and reported, "He's mad because they made him go outside to smoke a cigarette," Check reported, as the flame of a lighter could be seen near the cigarette.

The man moved around a little as he smoked his cigarette, then he turned in Blue Jay's direction and flipped the still lit cigarette into the grass not far from where Blue Jay was laying. He turned to go back into the building, but then stopped and turned back. Blue Jay and the Team thought that maybe he saw something, as he and the long range shooters put a little pressure onto their triggers.

"He's bitching about his superior inside again," Check alerted everyone. "He's just picking up the cigarette, so the bastard inside won't complain about that."

While still bitching, the man picked up the cigarette butt, then went back inside the building.

All was quiet for several hours, then Check's voice came over the com. "It sounds like they're stopping for the night."

"I don't like Blue Jay being in that exposed position, especially since he doesn't know they'll be coming out," JC said over the com. "I'm going out to reel him in." He started to move.

"Let me do it," Bean requested. "I still owe that peckerhead one from the Tortuga Project."

JC agreed with a smile and Bean moved quickly toward the building while Check kept him informed about what was going on inside the building.

As Bean got close to the building, he moved very quietly until he was up close behind Blue Jay. He extended his MP5 and tapped the end of the barrel on the bottom of his boot harder than was necessary.

That startled Blue Jay who quickly turned and saw Bean's smiling face. Knowing it was time to go, he quickly and quietly removed the com unit from the vent, then both men crawled to the back of the house to a position further away and waited.

"You didn't have to scare the shit out of me," Blue Jay complained.

"Paybacks are a bitch. Remember all of that Mr. Stealth shit you gave me on Tortuga?" Bean replied.

"You always were a peckerhead," Blue Jay replied as they continued to watch the building as the men filed out.

The last man to leave the building went to the area where Blue Jay had been laying, bent down, and reached behind the power meter. After that, he also headed for the house.

"Good call, JC," Jockey said over the com.

As everyone waited for the house to go dark and quiet down for the night, JC was on the com. "The last man out went to the power meter then reached behind it. Maybe some sort of security system."

Blue Jay was again on the com and reported, "There's a switch next to the vent. Was wondering if it had something to do with security."

After everything was quiet, the two moved back to the building, turned off the security system, and while Bean kept watch inside the door, Blue Jay searched for and quickly found the entrance to the underground room. After photographing everything, he could find the duo left the building, turned the security system back on, and rejoined the Team. After moving to another location, surveillance was re-established to see if any activity occurred after they had departed their original location.

Two hours later, JC was on the com and the Team departed the area.

Chapter 11

The following day, the Teams, Mac, and JJ were busy preparing everything that was collected at the Farm for analysis.

Check made an English version of the recording. All pictures of the documents were blown up to a larger size and were displayed around the meeting room and on folding tables that had been put up.

Once everything was ready, JC announced, "Let's all have a seat." With everyone seated, he said, "Before we start reviewing the material, JJ will give an update on the Board's research into the shipping company."

JJ stood up and said, "As we all know, the shipping company is a front, but checking for a paper trail did pay off. The shipping company has one small freighter registered in Malta and that begs the question why create a dummy company that has a real ship? The answer could be to make it easier to gain access to ports, and in this case, probably ports on the east coast.

"U.S. Intel is aware of the situation and is trying to locate the ship so the Navy can pay them a visit, but so far have been unsuccessful."

"Maybe the ship's name will show up somewhere in the photographed documents and give us an idea about its current location," JC suggested. "But first, I'll bring JJ, Mac, and the House Team up to date prior to starting the analysis."

After bringing the five up to speed, JC addressed everyone by saying, "Here's how I would like to proceed. Check created an English version of the recording we managed to get at the Farm last night and copies are available for you all to analyze, but first, he'll walk us all through the original recording, translating, and stopping at points where he feels their voices may have revealed something important. After that, we will all examine the documents on our own, then reconvene, and go over the documents of interest as a group, discussing each one as we go."

JC then turned the meeting over to Check for the walk through. "If anyone has a question during the run through, please don't wait to ask it. I'd rather answer the question while what was said on the recording is still fresh in everyone's mind." He then started the review of the recording.

It became obvious during the running of the tape why a shipping company cover was being used. More than one reference was made about the ship. Toward the end of the recording, the word 'Shebec' was heard and Bris raised his hand for a question.

After Check stopped the tape, Bris inquired, "What does Shebec mean?"

"Shebec is the name of a type of ship. It was liked and used by Barbary Pirates. At first pass, I'd say it's probably the reason these terrorists are using that name when referring to their ship."

Having answered the question, Check restarted the tape and a short time later, had finished the initial run through.

JC stood and said, "We'll break for lunch and then reassemble to analyze the photos of the documents."

After lunch, the Teams were back in the meeting room going over all of the photos or listening to the English version of the recording.

Tic seemed to be very intent on one of the photos and was looking at it with the aid of a magnifying glass. "See something?" JC inquired.

"Probably nothing, but wondering why this is written so small?" Tic explained.

"Check, Tic has a question," JC announced.

"Xebec and the numbers 3763?" Tic inquired.

"That's pronounced 'Shebec' and the word mentioned on the recording," Check added, as he moved toward Tic followed by Bris.

"Wonder why is it written so small on the document?" Tic wondered aloud, as Check and Bris also started studying the document.

Hours had passed and except for a dinner break, everyone kept analyzing the photos of the documents and the recording.

"I'm getting punchy," Jockey admitted, "and I know we're dealing with a ship, but what is 'drift test successful' all about?" he questioned, as he held up a photo for all to see.

"Ship and drift do go together, but what if in this case they don't?" Jockey questioned.

"Let's kick it around," JC advised. "What drifts?"

"Things drift on water," LadyA started.

"Glide is another word for drift. Maybe a glider is involved?" Met offered.

"Coast is another. Maybe some sort of unmanned vehicle is part of the plan," Pru spoke up.

"Things also drift on the air," Benz said in a normal voice.

"What was that, Benz?" JC said, asking him to repeat what he had just said.

"Things drift or float on the air," Benz said louder.

"I think you just nailed it," JC said with everyone else agreeing.

"Maybe we should start an analysis board to see if any of these items look like they go together," JC suggested, as he removed some of the pictures covering the chalkboard. In the first column, he wrote Ship, The Rising Moon, and then Xebec 3763 underneath each other. Second column was Drift Test was Successful and underneath that heading wrote Things Drift on the Air.

"Anything else?" JC inquired.

"Maybe we should have a column for the man from the shipping company," Blue Jay offered. "It was established he visited the Farm, but not the reason why."

JC shook his head in agreement, as he took down pictures that had been hung in front of the chalkboard so he could add more columns.

"He would have made a good schoolmarm," a voice observed.

"Uncle Donald's one-room schoolhouse," another voice said.

"There's an old saying, buy them pencils and paper, send them to school, and they will probably eat the erasers," JC replied, still taking down the pictures.

While exchanging one-liners with the Team, he added the additional column and when finished, stood back away from the board, double checking everything, then asked, "You eraser eaters have anything else?"

After several more columns were added, JC inquired, "Anyone else?" When no one spoke up, he added, "I'm sure these columns will have many entries added to them in the next day or so."

"Is everyone ready for a break and some refreshments?" JC asked.

"Yes, Uncle Donald," more than one voice replied.

JC looked at Mac and said, "Ten years ago, when we created this Team, we had a good thing. Now, it has evolved into Huey, Dewey, Louie, and the Eraser Eaters."

"I keep trying to tell you that," Mac replied with fake sincerity.

"Looks like Uncle Donald recruited Phineas Mac Duck," an anonymous voice in the group observed.

"Since they're outnumbered and to make it more interesting, maybe the House Team should side with JC and Mac," Lady1 suggested to Top and LadyA who shook their heads in agreement.

If anyone was counting on a restful break, they were at the wrong place, as one-liners flew around the dining room like rounds being fired from an M-60 machine gun.

It wasn't restful, but it sure took their minds off the analysis they had been doing all day and would allow them to look at the material with a clear head when they returned to it.

Bris, Tic, and Check were the last three to turn in that night. They had written Soltam K6 on the board with a question mark after it, but by that time, they were too exhausted to do any research on it.

The next morning, when everyone was filing into the meeting room, JC said, "That looks familiar. If memory serves, it's the ID for a 120 mm mortar."

"That mortar is made by a private company in Israel, but since it's used by over a dozen countries, it wouldn't be hard to get one," Mac added.

"Could be some sort of an attack by sea and it would make it easier to move around a three hundred pound 120 mm mortar, but what sort of target could justify all of the elaborate planning, expense, and since it would have no way of escaping the U.S. Navy, the sacrifice of a cargo ship?" JC questioned.

"What are these bastards up to?" Mac said aloud, as he walked to the chalkboard and stood there thinking, staring at Soltam K6. "You know, in the U.S. military, we think in terms of high explosive or a long lasting flare fired from a mortar that can turn night into day, but what if they plan to use some sort of gas or nerve agent like Saddam used against the Kurds?"

JC added a 120mm Mortar column while Mac talked. Then he added Gas or Nerve Agent underneath the column.

"Let's summarize our columns," JC suggested. "A ship by the name of The Rising Moon. Possible codename Xebec or Shebec. The words Drift Test was Successful, and finally, 120 mm mortar that can use gas or nerve agent shells.

"The ship could sit offshore or in a harbor and lob in 120 mm gas or nerve agent shells, create an airburst, and let the agent drift on the wind, dispersing it over a large area."

"A small cargo ship could navigate waterways like the Potomac River, but hopefully in that case, it would be intercepted long before it got to the Washington, D.C. area."

"Let's get the east coast maps from the Com Shack and display them around the room," he then instructed.

"I better call a board meeting for tomorrow to share these findings," JJ said to Mac.

"Are they all still in the area?" Mac inquired. "Some said they may be traveling during the holidays."

"Yes, I know, but when this Project started to take off, they all canceled their plans and are staying in the area."

That said, JJ informed JC that he and Mac were going to the house to arrange a board meeting for the following morning, but they would return.

When JJ and Mac returned, many possible targets on the east coast had been considered, then most were discarded due to access by waterway or other factors, but the small list of possible targets was growing.

When JC saw the two men returning from the house, he asked, "Mac, the range of the 120 mm mortar is about four miles, but the Iranians have a rocket assist shell. Do you have an idea about its maximum range?"

"Think it's about ten thousand five hundred meters," Mac replied.

"Look at Phineas Mac Duck spit out the answers," Panda remarked.

"Go, Phineas," Jockey added.

"Ten thousand five hundred meters is about six and one half miles for the edification of you, Eraser Eaters," Mac said, as he saluted the Team with a smile on his face.

JC laughed at the exchange as he ran a string across the ledger at the bottom of the map and marked off 4 and then 6½ miles on the string. By placing one end of the string on top of a possible target, then checking where 4 and 6½ miles was marked on the string, it would show them the general location of the maximum range for a standard 120mm mortar and a rocket assist shell.

Once the Teams had isolated possible targets, they addressed their provability factor, but one city went to the top of the list and stayed there: NYC.

Before bringing to an end what had turned out to be very long days, JC inquired, "Any additional questions or concerns?" With none, JC ended the meeting.

———————

Five days had gone by since Dunn had passed all of the analysis the Teams had prepared to Di Flippi. The photographs of the documentation were held back for security reasons. If they were seen and questioned at CIA, it could be a problem for Di Flippi to explain, especially since the CIA wasn't supposed to operate on U.S. soil.

As for the analysis part, Di Flippi knew Major Tex and the Seal would have no problem getting up to speed with the material and then say they had done the Intel analysis. They were two of his best people that he could always rely on, especially if he kept them away from the Brit.

Chapter 12

On the morning of December 22, Mac and JJ had just entered the kitchen where Top, LadyA, and Lady1 seemed to be planning something.

"What are you three up to?" JJ inquired.

"Just contingency plans," Top replied. "In case we have Christmas dinner here."

"I thought both Teams had holiday plans and would be leaving today after the morning meeting?" Mac questioned.

"That's the plan, but just want to be prepared. You know how those Eraser Eaters can be," Top explained.

"Tell me about it," Mac laughed, then all started moving toward the door and the morning meeting in the Barn.

Everyone was already seated when the five arrived, so JJ went to the front of the room while the others found seats.

"Morning all and Merry Christmas," JJ started and all wished him the same. "I'm sure you're

132

anxious to get on your way, so I'll be brief. Since the Federal people are involved, that puts us on the sidelines again. The Board, Mac, and I would like to thank you all for another job well done and they want me to convey a Merry Christmas to you all. With that, I wish you all a safe journey and an enjoyable holiday season."

"Question," JC spoke up. "Has the ship been found yet?"

"As of yesterday morning, The Rising Moon has still not been located," JJ replied.

"When you say 'we're on the sidelines again,' does that include not being able to go out for plane or boat rides?" JC inquired.

"I can see where this is going," JJ said, then inquired, "What do you have in mind?"

"A group our size can cover only one area and we all agree where that area is and why it was selected. Sooo, if we just happened to be in that area and see something, it would be our duty to report it to someone who has a connection with let's say someone in Washington, D.C."

"It looks like Uncle Donald has joined forces with Huey, Dewey, Louie, and the Eraser Eaters," Mac said to Top Kiner.

"So, you're saying the Team will not be going on leave?" JJ questioned.

"We all feel the Project isn't completed yet," JC replied.

JJ then looked at Top. "I didn't know. We were planning for Christmas dinner just in case."

"Well, I guess that brings us to my usual, 'How do we proceed,' question?" JJ told the Teams.

JC and the Team already had a plan worked out and immediately started briefing JJ, Mac, and the House Team.

New York City was always at the top of the list of possible targets, so after analyzing all of the Intel and proving it should be at the top of the list, they ran reverse analysis to try to prove why it shouldn't be at the top of the list with the same result.

After JC had explained how they decided on New York City, he went into the plan of action.

"First, we'll go into recon mode. Using an innocent looking single-engine aircraft with some sort of sightseeing business ID on the plane, we'll monitor the waterways around the New York City area. We ran exercises called, How would you do it? where the Team played the part of the terrorists, and may I say, I'm glad these people are on our side. We will monitor the entire area, but will focus on the Raritan Bay area."

The following day, the poor man's SR-71 was again in the air, busy checking the waterways around New York City. While Jockey attended to flying in the busy skies around NYC, JC and Mac used binoculars and spotter scopes to ID every ship they saw. Having completed a loop around Manhattan Island, the plane entered the Raritan Bay area and their primary focus.

After identifying the ships that were at anchor in the bay, Jockey headed toward a smaller craft sitting by itself.

"Is it cold down there?" Jockey inquired over his com unit.

"Get knotted," a British accent quickly replied.

"Such language," Jockey replied, then said, "Uncle Donald, do you want me to turn up the heater a little?"

"This might be a good time to test that shoulder held anti-aircraft weapon," Panda suggested.

JC and Mac thought the exchange was very funny, especially since the heater in the plane wasn't working and they were probably colder than the people on the boat.

"We have to go now," Jockey informed the boat. "Someone just told me where they make a great Irish coffee," but in fact, the plane had to go to refuel. He then banked the plane to the left and headed toward the entrance of the bay.

The remainder of that day was uneventful, as was December 24, the following day, until Benz reported, "There's a ship entering the bay."

All eyes focused on the entrance and closely watched a cargo ship that was slowly making its way into the bay.

Blue Jay got onto the radio and simply said, "Is your grandmother coming to dinner tomorrow?"

"I don't know, will check and get back to you," Jockey replied after hearing the phrase that alerted him a ship had been spotted. Jockey quickly navigated the plane to leave Long Island Sound area and returned to the bay.

By the time the plane had arrived, the cargo ship had made its way to the far left side and had dropped anchor in the New Jersey part of Raritan Bay.

It was decided that the plane would approach the ship from the south, pass over it, proceed north for a while, then turn 180 degrees and make a second pass over it. It was just a sightseeing aircraft with a large Happy Holidays banner trailing behind.

Since the plane would only pass over the ship twice, efforts to take pictures were moving at a furious pace.

Once the plane had passed over the ship for the second time and was heading south again, JC said, "The name isn't the Rising Moon, but I have a gut feeling that's the ship."

"I agree," Mac confirmed, "and there are tarps on deck covering something, but I can't tell what," he added, hitting rewind on his video recorder for another look.

It was a good call by JC and Mac. After the firefight in Malta, the ship was notified by radio to change the name of the ship to The Sea Merchant.

JC had dialed a number on his cell phone and when Tic answered, he said, "Hi, I just wanted to remind you to bring your camera for the Christmas Eve celebration tonight."

"I have it sitting by the door, so I wouldn't forget it," Tic assured him, as Check held one of the cameras they were going to install closer to the car door. Tic gave Check the finger, as he said a few more words to JC then hung up.

Since the two were alerted when the ship entered the bay, they had already selected where the cameras would be positioned and were waiting at the first location for JC to give the go ahead.

As the two got out of the 4x4, Tic said, "It's colder than a rat's ass out here."

"You can say that again," Check agreed.

"It's colder than a rat's ass out here," Tic said again.

"Very funny," Check said, holding back a smile. "Maybe I should have said, 'I don't know how cold a rat's ass gets, but since you seem to be an expert on the subject, I'll take your word for it.'"

"You know, we have to work on your one-liner comebacks," Tic replied. "Instead of one sentence, you seem to reply with a paragraph. Sometimes they're so long, I forget what the original one-liner was."

"Kafca," was Check's one-word reply.

"Kafca?" Tic inquired.

"Kiss a fat cow's ass," Check said, then inquired, "was that reply short enough for ya?"

"That's not nice. Remember, I'm part Hindi on my mother's side," Tic responded.

"You're full of shit. I met your mother," Check corrected.

"Oh, yeah, I forgot about that," Tic acknowledged. "Well, anyway, I'm glad to see you're getting better at the one-liners."

After Tic rappelled down the face of the cliff and placed camera one, Check positioned camera two at a different location, once again involving rappelling.

Tic and Check were both wearing com gear, so while one was installing a camera, the other was relaying instructions about positioning from the Ladies who were watching video screens back at the Com Shack.

With the two cameras in place and working properly, everyone started heading for the Barn and some much-needed warmth.

As everyone returned to the Barn, JJ, Top, Lady1, and LadyA were there to first greet them and then to get them involved with the little Christmas celebration they had organized.

When Tic and Check arrived, they were first greeted and then Top inquired, "I'll bet that wind was cold coming off the bay. Let's get something to help you thaw out." Then led them to where hot food and drinks were set up.

Jar Head, Doggie, Swabbie, and their wives were invited to spend the holidays with JJ, Mac, and the Teams, and were enjoying themselves at the party.

After about two hours, Jar Head said to Doggie and Swabbie, "Let's go check out the Com Shack."

"Ain't technology wonderful?" Jar Head said loudly, as the three looked into the Com Shack.

Blue Jay looked, took out his cell phone, dialed a number, and then said, "Three ancients seem to have wandered away from the party."

"The ancients again?" Doggie observed.

"It's all your fault. You didn't train him right," Jar Head said.

"You keep saying that, but he was yours," Doggie corrected.

"Was he? Guess I'm just trying to forget," Jar Head explained, as Blue Jay flipped him the bird while watching the video screens.

A few seconds later, Bean entered the room and Doggie said, "Now here's the one I trained. You can tell just by looking at him he's better trained and more respectful than yours."

Bean just flipped Doggie the bird in response.

"I guess all of that respectfulness doesn't apply to arm and hand signals," Jar Head observed.

"It's all my fault. I never should have let you two recruit your replacements when we worked at the Agency."

This was new. Swabbie usually didn't get involved in the verbal skirmishes between these four and when he realized all four men were looking directly at him, he quickly added, "Or not."

"So, what's the scoop with this?" Jar Head inquired.

"We decided Team members would take a one-hour shift to watch the ship around the clock."

"So, what are we, orphans?" Doggie asked.

"We figured since it was the Christmas holidays, we wouldn't bother you," Bean answered.

"See, I told you mine was the good one," Doggie poked Jar Head with his elbow.

"You always were a kiss ass," Blue Jay informed Bean.

"I was just telling them why," Bean started to explain, but was cut off by Blue Jay. "No, no, you always tried to be teacher's pet ever since forever."

"Screw you," Bean snapped back. "You and all of your stealth training. I'll bet that training came in handy when you snuck over and kissed the teacher's ass when we were in training."

"So, does this mean we're included in the watch?" Jar Head inquired.

"See, JC?" Blue Jay told him.

"Yeah, he'll put you into the lineup," Bean added.

While walking down the hall, Jar Head said, "We still got it."

"Yeah, they'll be going at it for a while, Doggie replied.

When the three were out of earshot, Blue Jay said, "Those peckerheads will never change. Get us fired up then leave chuckling."

"I guess this play acting we do gives them a little joy?" Bean observed. "But I do think you could have gone with 'You always were a kiss ass' or 'teacher's pet since forever,' but not both."

"So am I working from a script over here?" Blue Jay inquired.

"And what was cutting me off with 'No, no' before I finished my bullshit?" Bean asked.

"Okay, I'm sorry," Blue Jay apologized, paused, then said, "that you were always a kiss ass and a teacher's pet since forever."

"That's it," Bean announced and the battle was really on.

When JC and Mac entered the Com Shack five minutes later, the two were still engaged in a verbal battle.

"Now what's this skirmish all about?" JC inquired.

"I think it all started with a visit from our Agency Fathers," the duo replied.

"Need say no more," JC said with a smile. "We're going to move these monitors into the big room so everyone can enjoy the party tonight, plus Christmas dinner tomorrow," as he and Mac held up the cable that would be used to complete the task.

"You children want to unhook one of those monitors while JC and I run the cable?" Mac requested.

Without hesitation, the two men turned off one of the monitors, unplugged the electrical cord, turned it around, and started to disconnect the cable. While the monitor was being disconnected, Mac and JC started running the first cable from the Com Shack to the big room.

Within 30 minutes, both monitors were hooked up in the big room and finishing touches were being performed.

"Does the party seem a little quiet?" Lady1 asked LadyA in a low voice.

"It's not bad as parties go, but it is a little quiet for this crowd," she replied.

"Shall we?" Lady1 asked, as she nodded toward the duo.

"We shall," LadyA confirmed.

Blue Jay and Bean were looking at the monitors when LadyA said, "Isn't this nice that we can all be together?" as she and Lady1 joined the duo.

"It does make a party more enjoyable when friends and loved ones can be together during the holidays."

That statement got JJ's attention and he quickly looked at Mac a short distance away.

"Sunny Sands anyone?" Mac said, as he raised his drink in a toast toward JJ.

Since Blue Jay and Bean picked right up on what they were up to, they escalated the Ladies' plan, whatever that was, and it turned out not to be a silent night.

———

Ship watching seemed to draw more than one pair of eyes at a time, even during the early morning hours. It was Mac's turn to watch the ship and JJ and both Teams joined him with coffee cups in hand.

"Are we all set up for transporting the Board to the Barn?" JJ inquired.

"We'll start the process around midday," JC answered.

JJ shook his head in agreement. Since the Board members had canceled their plans, but had sent their families on ahead to enjoy the holidays, JJ thought it would be nice if the Board joined them.

"I invited the Board to join us for Christmas dinner, especially since it looked like Top had already planned for it," JJ said.

"I didn't know anything, just wanted to be prepared," Top confessed.

Christmas dinner at the Barn was a very pleasant event. After General Mac led everyone in a prayer of thanks, they started to enjoy the outstanding dinner Top, LadyA, and Lady1, with the help of the others, had prepared.

When everyone had finished and were enjoying an after dinner drink, JJ stood, held his glass up high, and announced, "I would like to propose a toast." When everyone had joined him, JJ continued with, "May God bless and protect all here. May the entire world soon enjoy peace and good will toward man."

Chapter 13

The following morning, JC was on watch and Mac joined him.

"So, when will we start the dance?" Mac inquired.

"Well, they dropped anchor on Christmas Eve and I'm sure they were more than a little tense that night and the following day. Today, they will probably start to relax and figure they are home free, so two days from now, we'll start the dance."

"I'm surprised Dunn and Di Flippi went along with your plan," Mac confessed.

"I guess they had no problem with the reasoning," JC answered, "if the numbers 3763 we found in the documentation at the farm represented the number of days since the 9/11 attack, there was a good possibility the next big attack would occur on December 31, 2011. When the ship entered the bay, New York City was their target and dropping anchor made it obvious their objective was probably Times Square on New Year's Eve."

"Has Di Flippi notified his people about the plan?" JC inquired.

"Hell no," Mac quickly answered. "Di Flippi and Dunn both agreed if Home Land Security found out about it, they might react in haste causing the terrorists to launch their attack and try to kill as many people as possible. Di will notify the appropriate people at the right time so the bureaucrats won't get involved and screw things up."

"Is this afternoon meeting still on?" Mac inquired.

"Yes, at fourteen hundred hours. That's two P.M.," JC added.

"Really?" General Mac inquired.

"Thought I would tell you just in case you gave your twenty-four hour military wristwatch to a freedom fighter."

"Don't say that so loud," Mac warned. "If JJ hears freedom fighters again, he'll go off his wig."

"How, and more importantly why, do you come up with those stories?" JC asked.

"It's what I do," Mac explained. "JJ and I have been having verbal battles since before they made up the word verbal. In fact, that's why they invented the word so we would have a name for it."

JC stopped watching the video screen, looked at Mac, and asked, "Do you remember back when we were out recruiting the Team and you thought it would be a good idea to sneak up on Blue Jay, but instead, he snuck up on us and said something like, 'Two senile old fucks that escaped from the home'? Well, I'm beginning to think the kid was half-right."

"See what I get for adding something to your life?" Mac defended. "You fly aircraft and take trips around the world in big corporate jets."

"Get shot at while I'm flying those aircraft, get into firefights around the world," JC replied.

"Well, that's the price you pay. You don't want everything for free, do you?" Mac reasoned.

As the two were going back and forth, JJ walked in and asked what they were battling about.

JC said without hesitation, "He's going on and on about freedom fighters."

"Ya, traitor, ya," Mac reprimanded JC. "You and that Top Kiner can't be trusted and you're both former Marines. If I didn't know better, I'd swear you had been in the Girl Scout reserves."

JJ shook his head and questioned, "Girl Scout reserves? Where did that come from?"

"JJ, I just realized Blue Jay had it all figured out about him ten years ago."

The battle continued, so JJ just took a seat and enjoyed the show.

Everyone was in attendance at the afternoon meeting JC had called. "Well, I'm sure you will all agree when I say this Project couldn't get any further away from the way we normally operate." Everyone shook their heads in agreement.

"Our next and hopefully last involvement with this Project will happen at daybreak on the morning of December 28. It would be idiotic for a group our size to try to stop a cargo ship; however, we could turn out to be the last resort for stopping it from going up the Hudson River. Pru, Met, Benz, Panda, Bris, Bean, and Blue Jay will be in a small craft sitting about a half-mile away from the ship, always maintaining full view of the front of the ship while the shooters and spotters target people and windows on the ship's bridge.

"Top, Lady1, LadyA, Tic, Check, Jar Head, Doggie, and Swabbie will be stationed on both sides of the entrance of the Hudson and will primarily assault the ship's bridge with the assorted array of shoulder fired rockets we managed to come up with.

"Jockey, JJ, Mac, and I will be in the plane and will attempt to drop thermite grenades on the roof of the ship's bridge that could cause some concern. As you all know, they are designed to eat through most anything and if they get onto the bridge, it will add to the chaos already being caused by rounds and rockets assaulting the bridge area. I realize it is super thin and hope it is not necessary, but just in case."

"Excuse me," Jockey said, as he raised his hand. "Do you really think we will do any damage to that ship by dropping thermite grenades on it?"

"Maybe if you added water-filled condoms to the bomb load it would do something," Panda suggested.

"Maybe if we pulled a condom over your head and added you to the bomb load it would be even better," Jockey fired back.

"Sorry, I can't. I'll be boating on the bay that day, but I'll try to catch your bomb run. Now, will that be before or after we attack the ship with .50 caliber rounds?"

".416 rounds," Pru corrected.

"I stand corrected, .416 rounds." Panda stood up, turned toward Pru, did a slight bow, and said, "Thank you."

Pru stood up, did the same, and said "My pleasure."

After more comments flew around the room, JC said, "Well, Mac, I'd say they're ready."

"Yeah, looks like it by the way these Eraser Eaters are sounding," Mac agreed.

"Correction, that's Huey, Dewey, Louie, and the Eraser Eaters, if you please," Bean corrected.

Mac just rubbed his head and said, "I've got to get a different job."

———————

At the crack of dawn on December 28, a pleasure craft was sitting about three quarters of a mile from the freighter. What looked like a large canvas just spread out over the deck was actually concealing a small hide where shooters and spotters kept watch on the freighter and were constantly ranging it. "I say, how are we going to stop that ship if it starts moving toward the Hudson River?" Pru inquired from under the canvas.

"First, we'll fire a warning shot across its bow. If they don't stop, the fight is on," Blue Jay answered.

"So, you think they'll see a .416 round splashing in front of the bow of a ship that size?" Panda inquired.

"Of course they will," Blue Jay confirmed with a smile.

"Custer in a small boat," Panda remarked, referring to Custer's last stand.

"More like frozen custard," Benz remarked, getting a chuckle from everyone.

After a pause, Met commented, "The way this boat is bouncing, we'll be lucky to hit any part of that ship."

"Quite so," Pru agreed.

"It is getting a little choppy," Blue Jay agreed. "Bris, do me a favor, go below and get those two gyroscopes and hand them to those two Mary's under the canvas. Apparently, they have lost their sense of adventure for long-range shooting."

"I say, are we the Mary's in question?" Pru asked Met.

"Seems so," Met confirmed then added, "I hope he didn't screw up the gyroscopes like he did the Michener Museum trip."

"Good show," Pru said to Met, then started to chuckle.

"Is there anyone on the planet who hasn't heard that story?" Blue Jay exclaimed.

"I think there are a few people on Guam who haven't heard about it yet," Panda offered.

"Do I have to remind everyone that Bean was driving that day?" Blue Jay announced.

"Don't bother me. I'm trying to figure something out," Bean replied.

"Already know I'm going to regret asking, but what are you trying to figure out?" Blue Jay inquired.

"Remember that two million dollars we seized on Grand Cayman? Well, if we had divided it evenly, each person on both Teams would have gotten $142,857 dollars."

"Here he goes again about dividing up the shit. Who are you anyway?" Blue Jay inquired.

"I say, actually, it would be 142,857 dollars and 14 cents," Pru corrected from under the canvas.

"And 14 cents," Bean quickly added.

"Oh, yeah, and how could I have forgotten your associate, Mr. Math Buster," Blue Jay said. "I thought you two gave up doing these little math mind melters?"

"Well, remember what happened to Thought. Thought, thought he farted, but he shit his pants," Bean replied.

"I'll be up on the bow wrapping something heavy around my neck if anyone wants me before I jump overboard," Blue Jay told everyone, as he headed forward.

"I think it was something we said," Bean observed.

"Do you really?" a voice from under the canvas inquired with a chuckle.

Everyone knew they were the last ditch effort to stop the cargo ship from going up the Hudson or East River. They couldn't sink it, but maybe they could make it run aground short of its target.

Ron Wootters

As the sun started to come over the horizon, a white Bell Jet Ranger helicopter made its appearance and was heading toward the cargo ship. Everyone immediately focused on it, then Benz informed everyone, "It has New Jersey State Police written on the side."

The ship had been swinging at anchor during the night and was now facing east, something that didn't go unnoticed by the helicopter, as it maneuvered, so it approached the ship from the direction of the rising sun.

When the Jet Ranger was close to the bow of the ship, it hovered and then over a loud speaker, asked the ship to identify itself.

Eventually, a man appeared on the side bridge of the ship with a handheld speaker and while trying to block the blinding sun with his other hand, complied with the request.

That done, the State Police helicopter informed the ship that it would be boarded for inspection purposes.

"And I always thought that, "One riot, one trooper" phrase was just a joke," Blue Jay said.

"Looks like he has a door gunner and maybe a few others onboard," Panda advised while looking through his spotter scope.

"While the Bell helicopter had their attention at the bow, NJSP boats from Marine Services were approaching the ship from the stern."

"What's causing so much dust on that island?" Jockey asked JC who swung his binoculars in the direction he was pointing.

After focusing, JC announced, "Six more State Police helicopters, two Bell Rangers, and four Sikorsky S-60's. Looks like the strike force will be made up of the New Jersey State Police Aviation, Marine, and the NJSP teams."

"This could go down easy, but in case the shit hits the fan, watch out for an asshole that may pop out of nowhere," Blue Jay instructed.

———————

Not being able to verify if The Sea Merchant was legitimate or was actually The Rising Moon, Di Flippi decided to follow that old adage, it's better to be sure than sorry. If the ship complied with the request for inspection, it would be carried out. If they wouldn't comply, the NJSP was aware of why they were challenging the ship and had arrived in force.

———————

The man on the side bridge wasn't sure how to react and had been joined by two others when someone on the ship spotted the approaching boats and sounded the alarm.

"There's an asshole running toward the bow and keeps pointing back," Benz notified Blue Jay.

"Probably about the boats," Blue Jay advised. "This will tell the tale."

The captain still seemed undecided on what to do when a man suddenly appeared on the main deck with a shoulder held rocket launcher and aimed it at the Bell helicopter.

"Take him out," Blue Jay ordered, but before the two shooters fired, the door gunner in the Bell helicopter took down the terrorist and the Jet Ranger took evasive action. As the helicopter dove down and made a 180 degree turn to get some distance between it and the ship, Benz alerted, "another one on the main deck at 9 o'clock."

The man on deck had the helicopter in his sights and as he started to squeeze the trigger, two .416 rounds picked him up and threw him several yards back, causing the rocket to miss the Bell Ranger, but close enough to get a, "That was close," out of the pilots.

When they came under fire, the five helicopters launched from Sandy Hook Island, plus more boats from NJSP Marine Police appeared, all heading toward the ship.

The Bell Ranger that came under fire performed another 180-degree turn and was heading back toward the ship with two additional members of the Teams now in the doorway ready to fire.

When it approached the bow, it again hovered, as the two other Jet Rangers did the same off the stern and port side, as the Sikorsky helicopters and NJSP boats approached.

The ship was in a state of confusion, but was starting to get organized, as one of the Sikorsky hovered over the bow while another did the same at the stern.

While the door gunners from the Bell Rangers gave cover, four members of the Teams quickly rappelled from two of the Sikorskys as four others from the boats climbed ropes that had been secured by firing crappling hooks onto the deck of the ship. After Team members from all four Sikorskys and the boats were on the deck, they proceeded to secure the ship. After two firefights on the main deck, the troopers started the more dangerous task of securing below deck and quickly, but cautiously completed that task.

With the ship secured, one of the Sikorskys moved into position and two additional men rappelled to the deck.

"I say, is that who I think it is?" Pru wondered.

"Yes, it's the Seal and Major Tex," Benz confirmed.

"How in the hell did they manage to get involved, especially since CIA isn't supposed to operate in the U.S.?" Bean asked.

Di Flippi had managed to get Major Tex and the Seal attached to Home Land Security, and since they both happened to be visiting in New Jersey for the holidays, they were the obvious choices to check out the ship for chemical or biological weapons. It would also give Di Flippi firsthand information before some bureaucrat started playing bullshit games about the Intel.

"Speaking of not supposed to be operating in the U.S., we better move on. They're going to come looking when they realize that terrorist was taken out by two .416 caliber rounds," Blue Jay advised, as he motioned for Bris to start the engine and to get underway.

As the boat headed toward the New York side of the bay, Bean announced that a NYC police boat was heading toward them.

"Somebody at Home Land Security must have alerted everyone or someone onshore called 911 about all of the activity around the ship," Blue Jay announced. "Continue breaking down that hide and fold up the canvas. Pru, Met, you know the drill for the 416's," and the two men started stripping down the weapons and dropping the parts over the side.

Jockey saw the approaching police boat and took a course not close, but within range of binoculars while JC and Mac kept watch of the boat.

"Ho, shit," Mac commented.

"What's wrong?" JJ inquired.

"I'd rather not say," Mac replied.

"You may as well," JC advised, "but be tactful."

"Okay, I'll be tactful," Mac agreed. "JJ, do you remember Charley Tuna, that freedom fighter in Cuba?"

The NYPD boat seemed to be heading straight for them and everyone was preparing for a stop and check, but the police boat didn't seem to be slowing down and seconds later, passed them on their starboard side.

"They must be responding to a 911 call from shore. If Home Land Security alerted them, they would have checked out all small craft. Keep your course and don't increase speed until they get further away," Blue Jay advised Bris. "Then increase speed gradually."

The plane stayed in the area until everyone had cleared the area, then Jockey headed for the small airport they were using.

Chapter 14

J started the morning meeting with, "I'll bring you all up to date about the assault on the Rising Moon yesterday. The ship was taken with no loss of life to the strike force, plus it was taken intact.

"No 120 mm mortars were found on the ship, but other parts of your analysis was right on the money, especially the drift test.

"Apparently, others had run tests over the past few years with different smells that would float on the air from New Jersey and cross over into Manhattan. I remember seeing something on the news, and I'm sure you all did as well, about a smell in Manhattan, but no one knew where it came from.

"The plan for the freighter was to proceed up the river on New Year's Eve and prior to the ball coming down, release a nerve agent that floats on the air and would be carried into Times Square by air currents that flow from the New Jersey side of the river. It goes without saying if the freighter was allowed to get into position and the plan had worked, a tremendous loss of life would have occurred from both the nerve agent and the results of a million people stampeding once people started falling."

"So that begs the question, what were those writings on the documents referring to?" JC questioned. "Were they part of the original plan and then taken out? Were they notes about another terrorist plot?

"The big question for the Team is, Should we put off going on leave and take a hard look into the matter?"

"Since we're all still up to speed with this Project, it may be the best time to do additional analysis," Jockey offered and everyone agreed.

With that said, JJ motioned JC to the podium and he continued the meeting with, "Tic, Check, and Bris had strong feelings about this from the start and continued doing research, so I'll ask them to gather their findings and present it to us when they're ready."

"No need to wait," Tic announced as he, Check, and Bris stood up.

"Very good," JC commended, as he motioned them to the front of the room.

"We seem to be having an outbreak of Teacher's Pet in the Team," Panda said so the three could hear him.

"I'll bet they have apples for the teacher, too," Jockey added. "Probably carry one around for emergency butt smooching."

Tic, Check, and Bris just gave the two the finger in unison, as they moved toward JC.

"Don't know about you, but I'm shocked!" Jockey said.

"Me, too," Panda agreed. "I'm telling. Teacher, teacher!"

When the three arrived at the front of the room, JC turned the meeting over to them and Tic started with, "I'll start with a little refresher. As you all know, the word Xebec, pronounced Shebec or Zi' bek, found written on one of the documents from the Farm, plus the word Shebec heard on the recording also from the Farm, made us wonder about the name, especially since it was the name of a smaller fast moving ship the Barbary Pirates used. At that point, we followed two trains of thought. It could be a codename given to the ship because Barbary Pirates used Shebec to do battle with U.S. ships in the past or it could be the codename for another smaller craft.

"That brings us full circle and two questions.

"Was Shebec the codeword for the freighter and why was '120 mm mortar written in the documentation, but none found on the freighter?

"Obvious answers are, the mortar was just a scribbled thought or it was in the original plan, then removed."

"Another answer may be, both words, Shebec and the 120 mm mortar, pertained to another smaller vessel and if that's the answer, we need to try to establish the what, where, and when for that terrorist attack."

"Since the freighter has been neutralized, do you all still have that same strong feeling about this?" Panda inquired.

"Think I can speak for the three of us when I say yes, we still have a nagging feeling about it," Tic answered.

"Then it would seem another thorough analysis of all of the material is in order," Panda observed with everyone in agreement, then all started moving to set up the analysis process they had originally established for the Project.

Hours had passed with everyone scanning every photo of the documents and listening to the recording over and over when JC called for a coffee break.

While everyone sat around having their coffee and taking a mental break, Mac said, "We have the word Shebec, a small fast moving ship the Barbary Pirates used. We also have the words 120 mm mortar. Since no mortar was found on the cargo ship, let me run something up the flagpole and let you all shoot at it.

"Let's say Shebec never did apply to the freighter, but to another smaller vessel. Let's also say the120 mm mortar never did apply to the freighter, but to the smaller vessel, and since 120 mm mortar weighs in at about three hundred pounds, the vessel couldn't be too small. So now, we have the makings of another plan using a mortar for the attack or we have what all of us are most concerned about, the second part of a two-pronged attack. Since the maximum range of a 120mm mortar using an Iranian rocket assist shell is six and a half miles, the question would be, where and how would a boat get into position to fire an airburst over Times Square on New Year's Eve?"

"So, you're suggesting Shebec is part of the original plan and they would fire the mortar at midnight during the fireworks display?" JC inquired.

"That would be the logical time to do it. The airbursts would look like part of the fireworks, plus if an average person saw them being fired, they would probably assume they were part of the fireworks display," Mac answered. "Since we only have a few days before New Year's Eve, maybe we should focus on those possible firing positions we already established and try to backtrack to the current location of another boat. It would have been positioned long before the event, so we would be looking for something outside the New Year's Eve security perimeter, but close enough to try to avoid detection en route to their firing position at midnight. What do you people think?" Mac inquired.

"Let's get at it," JC instructed and everyone again attacked the Intel that was gathered from the Farm.

"I always said you weren't as dumb as what you look," JJ told Mac, as he stood and moved with the others.

"Excuse me!" Mac replied, as he followed JJ.

First using the max range of the 120mm mortar as a guide, they established what they thought would be the best locations to launch an attack on Times Square. With that established, the best approaches to that location were analyzed and then the possible areas where the boat could be positioned.

Hours of analysis had passed when JC got everyone's attention. "Since we're pressed for time, I think it best we conduct mini-meetings to discuss our findings to that point and to maybe narrow down our search area."

When everyone was seated, JC started the meeting.

"Since the freighter's approach would have been from the bay traveling north up the Hudson River, let's consider that route not a good choice. A second boat could have followed the same route then turned up the East River, but if the freighter was discovered, the area would have been flooded with police and they may have also gotten challenged.

"My guess is the route would be from the north, Hudson River or East, Long Island Sound. Like Mac said, the craft was probably positioned months ago outside any security perimeter that would be in force during the holidays."

With only a few days until New Year's Eve, it was decided since Long Island Sound was much larger, everyone would continue analysis on that area and at first light, Jockey, JC, and Mac would fly over and photograph suspected areas north on the Hudson River.

By the time the sun came over the horizon, the plane was approaching the area of interest from the analysis. They would first make a pass along the eastern shore so both JC and Mac could look for anything suspicious. Once that was completed, Jockey would turn 180 degrees and the western shore would be checked. With Mac armed with a video camera and JC with a camera equipped with a powerful telephoto lens, the two documented all suspicious sites.

Having completed their mission, they returned to the airport and then to the Barn. As the three men entered the Team meeting room, JC asked, "Find anything interesting?"

"Not really," Blue Jay answered. "How about you?"

"Have a few we're wondering about," JC replied. "Mac will show you all the video while I develop these pictures."

Several minutes later, Mac and Jockey were narrating the video that was taken earlier and pointing out their sites of interest. "I will not tell you which one, but the three of us agreed that one of these sites stood out from the rest," Mac told everyone.

By the time the video tour was completed, JC appeared with the photos. "I enlarged the pictures for better analysis," he explained, as he and a few Team members hung up the pictures around the room.

Armed with magnifying glasses, everyone analyzed the pictures.

Thirty minutes into their task, Bris said, "If you look at the front corners of this building, you can tell the side facing the river has been renovated. And if you follow the corners down to the bottom, they seem to be just hanging at water level. This house has been renovated by someone who didn't know what they were doing or it's a wall to cover up a pre-existing opening to the river."

The other Team members came over to investigate, then Benz offered, "There's something out of place about it. Do you have any other shots of the building?"

"A few," JC said, as he went into a large envelope and produced a handful of enlarged pictures of that house. "This is the one that stood out for Jockey, Mac, and I, but we wanted you all to get a fresh look and your opinions."

Everyone examined the new pictures and other things were noticed like an antenna that could possibly be used for overseas communications.

After hours of analysis, JJ got everyone's attention. "I know what the general consensus about this building is, but do you all feel we should move on this building? Keep in mind we're short on time and this would probably be our only shot at finding a boat that will be used in a mortar attack, if in fact one does exist."

After JJ had spoken, everyone went into deep thought about what he had said. They were running out of time, there were a few more sites on the Hudson that were also suspicious, plus the larger area in Long Island Sound hadn't been photographed yet.

JJ could see his question was one they didn't want to answer quickly, so he suggested, "Why don't we all take a break and reconvene in about an hour?"

Chapter 15

The Hudson River had a lot of activity this 2011 New Year's Eve, especially with people heading down river to watch the fireworks display at midnight.

Some had started their New Year's Eve partying during the afternoon and probably should have had a designated boat captain for their cruise down the Hudson that night, but by the looks of what their boat probably cost, if they hit anything, they would probably just buy it using pocket change.

That scenario really applied to the seven men on a luxurious craft that was making its way south toward New York City and the fireworks display. It was only 6:00 P.M., but at the rate they were moving, it would take six hours for them to get there.

The seven were definitely party animals, singing, blowing horns, whishing everyone a Happy New Year, and stopping from time to time to ask people to join them in a celebration drink.

It looked like the boat was going to bypass a building when a voice on the boat yelled out, "Hey, there's a building," as if it was somehow different from the other three they had just visited.

The motors were put into reverse and the boat backed up. After almost sideswiping the building, the men started yelling, "Hello, Happy New Year!" and banging on the side of the building to get the attention of anyone inside.

The people inside of the house were first alarmed, but then realized it was just drunken men, so someone went outside to get them to leave while others in the building looked on.

Since the two men standing at the front of the building were also looking at the drunks on the boat, it was easy for Blue Jay to approach from the left side, blend into the darkness, and then gain access into the building. Once inside and since the drunks on the boat were not taking no for an answer, he quickly moved to the lower level in search of Shebec.

The man who went outside finally convinced the drunks to leave and the boat slowly moved away from the building to continued its journey south or to the next house, whichever came first.

"Who were those bozos?" Panda said softly into his com unit.

"Maybe we should call 911 and make a noise pollution complaint," Jockey replied. "They're destroying Auld Lang Syne."

"Phineas Mac Duck may want to invest in some singing lessons," JC suggested as Mac, JJ, and the Board continued their merriment down the Hudson.

It didn't take Blue Jay long to discover what he was looking for and then he retreated to a dark corner of the building. Once there, he whispered the prearranged signal "Diamond," into his com, paused, then said, "Two, say again, two."

If Blue Jay found nothing, he and the Team would have departed the area, hoping an attack would not take place at midnight.

When JC heard the word diamond, he quickly dialed numbers on the cell phone already in his hand.

After one ring, a voice said, "Hello?"

"Diamond," JC said, paused, and then said, "Two."

"Happy New Year," Gil Dunn said while an off-key version of Auld Lang Syne bellowed in the background.

Dunn then called Di Flippi who was already up to speed on the situation and just needed to hear the word before alerting Home Land Security and the FBI.

The fact there were two caused some concern for Dunn and Di. It was obvious that each had a separate destination and may be difficult to locate both if they were allowed to get underway and that fact hadn't escaped the concerns of the Team either.

They were on U.S. soil and since the powers that be were probably already trying to figure where those .416 rounds came from that took out that terrorist on the ship, it was advisable a low profile be maintained.

Thirty minutes had passed when Blue Jay's voice was again on the com. "Hear some activity. Going to check it out."

Two street people pushing grocery carts were walking past the building. When they got to the front and after a brief conversation, they decided to approach the two men standing out front and ask for New Year's Eve contributions. The two men saw them coming and immediately told them to stop and leave while making gestures for them to continue walking past the building.

The street people weren't going to be dismissed that easily and kept walking toward the two men. When they got close, the men stepped forward and forcibly pushed them. Both gave way to the pushing and then pushing turned into throwing, as Benz and Panda threw the two men into the air and then dispatched them after they hit the ground (a different type of stealth).

Observing this on security monitors inside the building, 10 armed men immediately rushed toward the entrance.

Benz and Panda didn't waste any time either, as the grabbed their MP-5's from the carts.

Six of the 10 men came out of the entrance firing their weapons. Benz and Panda took out four and two others were taken down by Pru and Met using .30-06 caliber rifles. Blue Jay came out of the shadows blindsiding the last two, knocking them off balance and almost sending them to the floor. While they were trying to regain their balance, he dropped the two men that were about to go out the door and then the two he had intercepted.

After quickly surveying the area, Blue Jay said, "Clear," over the com.

Hearing the word, Benz and Panda joined Blue Jay inside while JC, Bean, Tic, Check, Bris, and Jockey quickly moved to the front of the building.

Once everyone was inside, JC assigned some of the Team members to check out the second floor while the others moved toward the boats Blue Jay had discovered.

The terrorists had emergency plans and activated them when the firefight broke out. A group assigned for defense took up positions behind the two boats while others prepared the boats to get underway.

The men assigned to check out the second floor had returned and the Team continued to move cautiously toward the rear of the building when Met came on the com. "You're getting company. Seven armed men in a van pulled up to the entrance of the building. Pru and I took out four, but three managed to get inside."

"I'll take it," Bean said over the com, already en route to the front of the building while inserting a fresh magazine into his MP-5.

Once inside, the three men continued to move very quickly toward the rear of the building and would try to get whoever was assaulting the building in a crossfire between them and the people protecting the boats, but two bursts from an MP-5 took two of them down. The third man dove for cover, as rounds from a third burst followed him.

"I don't have time for this shit," Bean mumbled, as he removed a grenade from his pocket, checked it out, then pulled the pin, and tossed it to where the terrorists had found cover. After hearing the telltale ping of a grenade spoon flying off and then seeing the grenade next to him, the terrorists picked it up and was in the process of throwing it back when Bean punched his ticket.

With the three terrorists neutralized, Bean walked over to the dead terrorists to retrieve the dummy grenade. It had a pull ring, spoon, and fuse, but no power inside. As he removed it from the terrorists' hand, he thought, *I picked up that trick from Blue Jay, but I would never admit it.*

Bean had just rejoined the Team when they heard a series of explosions followed by what sounded like the side of the house sliding into the Hudson.

"Sounds like they rigged the house for a quick escape for the boats," JC alerted over the com, and everyone knew when the debris sank deep enough to avoid fouling the propellers, the boats would get underway.

The drunk boat was now sitting down river and acting as the last line of defense in case the terrorists' boats got away. Foxie kept their boat parallel to the expected escape route while the other Board members stood along the deck with automatic weapons at the ready. The Board members performed very well during other Projects, so getting past them would not be an easy task.

With this new sense of urgency, JC was about to give the order for an assault when Bean said, "Why don't we give them something to think about first?" as he produced one of those old type frag grenades, a real one, that Jar Head and Doggie liked so much.

After Blue Jay produced another and all of the Team members were alerted, Bean and Blue Jay pulled the pins on the grenades then looked at JC. After taking a quick look at the enemy, and then making sure everyone had their heads down, he gave the word and the duo tossed the grenades while JC fired bursts from his MP-5 to keep the terrorists busy while he counted, "One thousand one, one thousand two, one thousand three," then he also ducked down. After two additional counts, the grenades exploded, but the boat on the right was already on the river and moving away from the building.The Team was outnumbered by the defenders, but the grenades took them by surprise and by the time they tried to regroup, it was too late, as the Team quickly disposed of them.

That done, all attention turned to the boat that had escaped.

The drunken boat was the last line, but not the only line of defense. Two other boats were sitting in the darkness on the Hudson in case something like this happened and Lady1 and Top Kiner raced to head off the escaping boat.

"Doggie, for the edification of you Army turds, this reminds me of the amphibious landings we used in the Marine Corp," Jar Head informed him over the com.

Seeing the two boats bearing down on them, the man behind the wheel of the terrorists' boat tried to escape and evade while others on the boat started shooting at the oncoming crafts. Lady1 wasn't about to back off and while the others on the two boats returned fire, she rammed the terrorists' boat, then after a brief firefight, the threat was neutralized.

"Well, I'm glad you finally got that out of your system. I've been worrying ever since you almost wiped out that yacht we were using during that Tortuga Island Project," Jar Head informed Lady1.

"At least this time it was the bad guy's boat and not one of ours," Doggie commented.

"That's sort of true. Remember, we had no time to waste to get into position, so that's a stolen boat that just rammed the enemy," Top Kiner corrected, as he pulled alongside the sinking craft to take on passengers.

Jar Head was the last to leave the boat and as Doggie helped him aboard, he inquired, "I didn't quite understand the last part of your Marine Corps Amphibious Landing?"

"Ask Swabbie," Jar Head replied. "Marines just make the landing, then fight. If there's a screw up during the ride in, it's the Navy's fault."

"Knew I should have declined the offer to come along," Swabbie replied.

With all of the people from the sinking boat onboard, Top Kiner was on the com as he continued to back away from the two sinking crafts. "You people all secure in there?"

"We're moving out now," JC answered.

"We'll hang out until you all get clear," Top replied.

Pru and Met were keeping close watch of the area and would also give cover to the Team as they departed the building.

After a quick exchange between JC and Pru, the Team left the building, then quickly disappeared.

"We're clear," JC said into the com.

"Roger that," Top replied, as he pushed the throttle forward, turned south away from where they had stolen the boats, and proceeded to where they had positioned transportation.

Top's boat didn't take long to cover the two miles to where the drunk boat was waiting until everyone had cleared the area.

As they passed, LadyA gave them a quick blink with a flashlight and got two blinks in return.

Due to security rules that were established when the Board and Teams were created, the two groups were kept apart, but that changed a little after the Board members talked JJ into letting them take an active part in a Project. After the first Project, the Teams knew the Board members were all good people, then after a second Project, plus a Bull Shit Derby Dinner, they all became lifelong friends.

———————

Everyone had arrived safely back at the Barn and were in the Team meeting room discussing and debriefing about the Project.

Ron Wootters

JJ and Mac sat in their usual seats in the front row when Mac informed JJ, "All weapons used for this last skirmish are present and accounted for. I know how upset you get over the cost of losing weapons during a Project."

"It's never been about the cost," JJ corrected. "What has to be done has to be done. It's those stories you keep coming up with about freedom fighters that are so dammed aggravating. Charley Tuna, Sunny Sands, and my personal favorite a freedom fighter on the deserted island of Tortuga."

"And all along, I thought it was about the cost," Mac said with surprise.

After a few minutes, Mac said, "JJ, on a serious note, I have to tell you something about Lady1."

Since JJ was concerned about the relationships between the Ladies, Blue Jay, and Bean, Mac had his undivided attention.

Overhearing the conversation, everyone in the room stopped what they were doing and watched as Mac and JJ continued their talk. It wasn't long before JJ's voice grew louder, saying, "I'll give you Lady1 used to be a freedom fighter and she sank a stolen boat," while getting Mac into a headlock.

"I guess that marks the official end of another Project," Bean announced and everyone shook their heads in agreement.

Chapter 16

The first two days of the New Year had passed with not much activity at the Barn, then on the third day, JJ called for a meeting.

With everyone once again seated in the Team meeting room, JJ began. "It seems like I'm always saying this and hope you all know it's still as sincere as the first time when I say the other Board members, Mac, and I want to again thank you for another excellent job, especially during the holiday season when I'm sure you all would have liked to have been somewhere else enjoying yourselves.

"At our meeting yesterday, the Board members again expressed how fortunate we are to have men and women like you."

"Put up your umbrellas, gang, have a feeling someone is going to shit on our time off parade," Panda alerted everyone.

"You got me," JJ confessed. "Guess I didn't want to hear the words myself. We would again appreciate it if you would delay your leave time.

The reason being, Di Flippi is already getting hounded with questions and would appreciate the people who actually did the deed to be close at hand with the right answers."

It was a good reason on two counts. First, if Di Flippi didn't come up with the correct answers, it would cause suspicion, maybe followed by an investigation and that wouldn't be good for anybody.

Second and the main reason, Di Flippi is good people and the Team liked him a lot.

After the Team agreed to postpone their leave, Blue Jay stood up and said with a very serious voice, "Since we are yet again being asked to postpone our leaves, plus the hardships we endured during the holidays and especially on New Year's Eve, I suggest while we're waiting," he paused, then said very quickly, "we have a Bull Shit Derby Dinner."

"Oorah," Mac endorsed the suggestion.

"Couldn't have said it better myself, Mac," JJ agreed. "Of course, we can have a Bull Shit Derby Dinner, but I do have one concern. Jockey, you tell us those messages you read and the points awarded at the dinner come from a super secret source that you don't even know about and your only connection with them are carrier pigeons."

"That's my story and I'm stuck with it," Jockey confirmed.

"With such short notice and with this winter weather, will it affect delivery of the messages?"

"I'm sure it won't, JJ," Jockey said with confidence. "These are all-weather pigeons and were trained at a secret hangar where I was trained."

"Crotch Airways, your old alma mater? Do the pigeons fly backward, too?" JC inquired.

"And may the pigeons bring messages containing many points for you at the Derby Dinner," Jockey replied, as JC laughed.

———————

The Teams, all of the Board members, Jarhead, Doggie, Swabbie, their wives, and Di Flippi were all in attendance at the Derby Dinner. After cocktails, everyone would sit down to dinner and enjoy the excellent food. After that it was anybody's guess how things would proceed, but one thing was for sure, it wouldn't be quiet.

Dinner had been served and everyone was enjoying an after dinner drink when Jockey stood and got everyone's attention. "We have an announcement and, of course, the awarding of points in the race for the JCCF Award, but first, according to this note someone left at the podium, Doggie claims he still doesn't understand the last part of that Marine Corps Amphibious Landing that was made on New Year's Eve. Jar Head claims the Navy was responsible. Swabbie said that couldn't be right because the people who drive the boats in the Navy are called a Coxswain and the driver of the boat that night may have swain, but she doesn't have a, well, you get the idea."

Doggie went further up the food chain seeking an answer, but all Mac said was, "Former freedom fighters can be unpredictable."

"So, I guess the answer is former freedom fighters like to ram other boats, unless JJ can clarify the matter for us."

JJ looked at Top and said, "Cancel that order for the big spoon, I'll need a small shovel."

"As you all know, we changed the award name to JCCF due to ladies now being present at the Derby Dinners. Well, three ladies anyway," Jockey continued.

"Is that asshole trying to say we aren't ladies?" a woman's voice inquired.

Everyone at the table immediately looked at Lady1 who was looking at LadyA with surprise, but then said, "Since we're changing roles, let me say, ho, my, is he saying we aren't ladies?"

"I don't sound like that," LadyA defended.

"To me you do and by the way, how come you got the 'A' and I got the '1' ?"

"Because I'm better," LadyA replied.

"Moving on," JJ advised, as Mac motioned for Jockey to quickly proceed, both remembering how they almost lost their sanity trying to get the codenames for the Ladies established in the first place.

"Onto the awarding of points," Jockey announced, "and the current point standings are, and as usual, please hold your applause until the end. JC—8, Blue Jay—6¼, Benz—6, Panda—5, Bean—6, Check—3, Tic—2, Bris—2, Pru—2, Met—2, Top—2, LadyA—2, Lady1—3, JJ—1½, Mac—2, Dunn—1½, Wilson—1½, Dawson—1½, Howard—1½, Foxie—1½, and Jockey—2."

When Jockey had finished, halfhearted applause and a lackluster, "Yeah," was heard.

"Now calm down," Jockey continued. "Here are the new point awards.

"Benz and Panda, one and one-half points each for taking out the security guards and then four others at the front of the building on the Hudson. However, there will be a one-quarter point deduction each for not returning the shopping carts to the market."

"I always said this shit was fixed," Benz announced.

"What do you expect from a turd who learned how to fly at Dick Airways," Panda added.

"That's Crotch Airways, by the way," Jockey corrected.

"I was being kind, Nancy," Panda replied.

"An additional one-quarter point deduction each for disrespecting the messenger, remainder one point each," Jockey continued, as Benz and Panda had a hearty laugh.

"JC, who kept the terrorists under fire at the house on the Hudson preventing them from getting to the grenades and tossing them back, one point. People have said he would have kept the terrorists under fire longer, but he probably forgot what came after one thousand three. One-quarter point deduction for disrespecting the messenger, remainder three-quarters of a point."

"I didn't say anything, yet!" JC defended.

"The message says you don't have to, they already know what you're thinking," Jockey claimed, as he held up a piece of paper then commented, "Boy, these message senders are smart."

"Lady1, for preventing the terrorists' boat from escaping by ramming it, two points or one point depending on the reason. Two points if due to bravery. One point if due to trouble in paradise. Not sure what that means, but I'm sure the all knowing message senders will make it clear later in these messages."

"Pru and Met, for making great long distance shots from a bouncing boat taking out a terrorist with a rocket launcher who was about to fire at the NJSP helicopter. One point each."

"JC and Mac, while babysitting the Teams, took out six drug runners who were about to open fire on Pru and Met, two points each.

"However, there will be a half-point deduction each for not having a current babysitting license."

"The man is a... What are the words I'm looking for?" Mac inquired.

"Dick wad," JC suggested.

"Those are the words," Mac confirmed.

"One half-point deduction each for conspiring to disrespect the messenger, one point total each.

"Blue Jay, for infiltrating the terrorists' house on the Hudson, establishing the boats were there, and then taking out four terrorists before they could get out the door to join the assault on Benz and Panda, two points.

"However, there will be a one-quarter point deduction for not reminding Benz and Panda to return the shopping carts to the market."

"What do you expect from a turd who learned how to fly at Pussy Airways," Blue Jay announced.

"That's Crotch Airways, by the way," Jockey corrected. "It use to be Pussy, but we changed it to Crotch. Don't you remember?

"One-quarter point deduction for disrespecting the messenger," Jockey continued, as Blue Jay mocked him.

"One-half point deduction for mocking the messenger."

"Half a point?" Blue Jay complained.

"Yes," Jockey confirmed. "Apparently, mocking is twice as bad as disrespecting. Don't blame me. I just follow the rules of the message senders. One point total."

"Bean, for taking on three terrorists by himself at the house on the Hudson and preventing them from possibly getting the Team into a crossfire. One and one-quarter points.

"However, there will be a one-quarter point deduction for not reminding Blue Jay to remind Benz and Panda to return the shopping carts to the market. One point total."

"This shit is fixed," Benz complained again.

"And now, the Crotch Airways graduate is reading minds, too," JC added.

"I always did have suspicions about those damn messenger pigeons," Blue Jay said.

Laughter followed every complaint, then Mac added, "I have to agree, it's to a point of total corruption."

"Total corruption?" JJ inquired, looking at Mac.

"I was feeling left out again," Mac replied with a smile.

"Please watch your criticism," Jockey warned. "Sometimes, they station a stoolpigeon in the area and we don't want to anger the message senders."

"Somebody throw a stool at that pigeon," Bean requested, followed by more laughter.

This part of the Bull Shit Derby Dinner usually got everyone riled up, but this time, they were really having fun.

Points given for this made up award had been going on for years and Jockey always managed to get the messages even during inclement weather.

When things started to calm down, Jockey announced, "Here are the new totals. JC—9 ¾ , Blue Jay—7 ¼, Benz—7, Panda—6, Bean—7, Check—3, Tic—2, Bris—2, Pru—3, Met—3, Top—2, LadyA—2, Lady1—5, JJ—1½, Mac—3, Dunn—1½, Wilson—1½, Dawson—1½, Howard—1½, Foxie—1½, and Jockey—2."

After more halfhearted applause and another lackluster, "Yeah," Jockey announced, "Calm down, calm down. We have something in the romance department to clarify.

"Rumor has it that LadyA and Lady1 are romantically involved with Bean and Blue Jay and after their first date, were already looking at kitchen cabinets and Andersen windows. Ladies, are the rumors true?"

"Yes, I guess you can say we're romantically involved," LadyA answered.

"How dreamy, and looking at kitchen cabinets and windows during their first date. What's next a trip to Finkles Hardware? I guess that's why people say Blue Jay and Bean are incurable romantics," Jockey observed.

"People also say they know their way around a crotch and they aren't talking about an airway," Lady1 replied.

Mac was taking a sip of water, almost swallowed the glass, and while he was choking on the water, JJ looked at Bean and Blue Jay for their reactions. When both blew kisses to the Ladies, he poked Mac with his elbow and said, "I told you something could come of this, Mr. Funnyman, with the remarks."

"If I had only known Lady1 was a former freedom fighter, I wouldn't have said a thing," Mac defended.

Lady1's remark added even more fuel to the occasion and kicked it up another notch.

Hours later, everyone was played out and even Peeka and Sandy had called it a night and were sacked out in a corner.

JC stood and said, "I would like to make an announcement." Having everyone's attention, JC continued. "After ten years, Mac and I have decided to call it a day. We both feel you all can carry on very well without us, but if needed, we will be available."

JJ was caught totally off guard by the announcement and inquired, "This is so sudden, are you serious?"

"Not really," JC replied, "but Mac and I were wondering if we should go out and get involved with people who know how to party. You people poop out after only about six hours," he said, looking at Mac for confirmation.

"Six and a half actually," Mac confirmed and the party found new life.

"We have to remember to keep these two away from Major Tex, the Seal, and the Brit," Di Flippi informed Dunn.

"Tell me about it," Dunn replied.

After things got rolling again, JJ stood up and got everyone's attention. "Since JC and Mac have us all awake again, I'd like to thank everyone for your continued dedication and excellent service."

"They say our country functions like a big pendulum that swings to the left and then back to the right never staying in the middle. Let's all pray the pendulum hasn't gotten stuck to the left and soon returns to the middle or a little to the right." He then held up his glass to make a toast and was joined by the others.

"May God bless America," JJ announced and everyone echoed, "May God bless America!"

Have gone on ahead to perform Recon:
Lt. Col. Dermott McDonald USMC
1st Sergeant Joseph J. Keener, Jr. USMC
Mr. Clarence Teddy (Sid) Smith Original Merril's
Marauders
Mr. Yoshisada Yonezuka (Yone)
Mr. Andy Domingo
Mr. Howard Powers
Sandy
Peeka